GW01464113

A

Denis Linehan is an international selling author. He had his first work published in 1974, and in the meantime has written six previous books, a number of manuals and several articles.

This book is based on litigation taken by him to the Supreme Courts of both Ireland and the United States, as well as to the European Commission on Human Rights.

The author is a first class honours graduate of the National University of Ireland. A Fulbright Scholar, he also holds graduate law degrees from both the University of Michigan and Harvard University. A qualified solicitor, Denis Linehan received the Society Prize for 1980 from the Law Society of Ireland. He is a qualified Arbitrator and a former Fellow of the Salzburg Seminar, Austria.

To: Michael D. Higgins, T.D.,
With Compliments and Best
Wishes
From: Denis Linehan
October 24, 1997.

By the same author

Books

And Nothing But the Truth
Harvard Law School in Court
Business and Commercial Law
Land and Conveyancing Law
Consumer Law
The Biblical Diet

Articles

Derivative Suits in American, English and Irish Law
The Public Interest Law Movement in the United States
Trade Marks and Passing Off. The Irish – E.E.C. Regime
Truth in Business, the Consumer Information Act, 1978

DENIS LINEHAN

A WAD OF NOTES
All Eyes on the Money

GEM BOOKS

Gem Books
22 Summerstown Grove, Wilton,
Cork, Ireland.
An imprint of Emerald Publications

This edition 1997

Copyright © Denis Linehan

The author reserves the moral right to be
identified as the author of this work

ISBN 0 952 58131 0 2

Set in Palatino

Printed and bound in the European Union

Contents

Prologue: Isolation

After being offered a place at Harvard in 1984, I was placed
under duress to leave my employment at University College Cork by a number of administrators at that college.
The people involved may have felt threatened by the
prospect of my returning to the university with a doctor-
ate obtained on sabbatical.

During 1985-1986, I was subjected to intensive duress.
I was told that *a gun was being put to my head,* and that I
would be undermined by demotion to tutorials unless I
cooperated with a retirement on health grounds. Attempts
were made to evict me from my office. In the same period,
students were encouraged to sign a petition of complaints
against my lectures. Attempts were made to openly invig-
ilate at my lectures. I was suspended from lecturing. It was
sought to involve me in a *trial by students* of spurious complaints deliberately garnered by senior university administrators. The internal procedures at the university to
dismiss me on health grounds were activated. Although
eligible for over two years sabbatical and a travel grant to
pursue the doctoral studies, I was refused both. The university solicitors maintained that I had been unable to ful-
fil my duties for a number of years, notwithstanding that
I had been promoted in 1983.

I sued the university in 1986 on foot of the unlawful mea-
sures that were being taken against me. These proceedings
were settled on the 9th of July, 1986. A decree for £40,000
damages in my favour was ruled on order of the High
Court. I was also to be paid my salary while on leave at
Harvard until June, 1987.

The settlement on the 9th of July 1986, was bitter. It barred me from U.C.C. and effectively denied me a reference.

In the event, certain university personnel did not see the
July 9, 1986, High Court settlement as finalising matters. A

senior U.C.C. administrator who had been discredited in the case soon afterwards got leave of absence to go to Temple University in the United States. He visited Harvard at least twice in the following nine months. His taking leave of absence at that time would have required the consent of the president and finance officer at the university.

In my first term at Harvard, I became acquainted with Gerard Quinn, the only other Irish student at the law school at that time. He was pursuing doctoral studies, and in Autumn of 1986 foresaw himself as spending considerably more time there to complete these studies. To his surprise, he was offered a job at U.C.C. from January 1987. This sudden change of plans caused him to move from Harvard at Christmas, 1986. I maintain that he was got out of the way by university administrators, who were planning to remove me from the graduate programme in the following months in a way that would cost nothing to Harvard.

The criminal acts directed at me at Harvard began shortly thereafter. I was hospitalised twice in the following six months, the last six months of my thirteen years employment at U.C.C.

Early in 1987, I became subject to a systematic process of savage retaliatory abuse at Harvard. This had all the hallmarks of liaison between senior administrators of U.C.C. and Harvard.

1 Woodpecker

Shortly after my return from Harvard, I summarised in a sworn deposition the abuse that had taken place:

"Between 1974 and 1986, I lectured at University College Cork and also practised law on an occasional basis.

For a number of years, relations between me and the head of the law department at University College Cork – a professor McMahon – had been strained, arising initially I believe from his wish to be involved in a book I was writing, and also from personality differences. Prior to 1984, professor McMahon had vetoed four applications for sabbatical made by me ...

It had been an ambition of mine to attend the Harvard graduate programme for many years ... Having been accepted, I again applied for sabbatical in Spring 1985 – I had been promoted a few months earlier and at that time was eligible for two years sabbatical in respect of twelve years of service. The application was again blocked – one reason given was that study for a Harvard S.J.D. was not an adequate research project! Also, basic rights of mine were infringed by professor McMahon at this time. I pursued the matter successfully in the Irish High Court, but existing bad relations were worsened as a result and some reputational loss occurred for individuals, although the defendant party was University College Cork. Since my return to Ireland last June, I have heard that professor McMahon has resigned his Chair.

One of my referees to Harvard, professor Leonard Wrigley – who holds a degree from Harvard Business School – indicated to me at the time that it was a small world and that University College Cork might try to ruin me as a result of the litigation. Professor McMahon had contacts with Harvard Law School. He was a graduate of the school in or about 1970. He was particularly acquainted with one or two of the faculty, in particular, professor C. Byse. Moreover, for a number of years, he had arranged that a J.D. candidate from the school teach a legal writing programme at University College Cork.

Events in the Period August–December, 1986

I commenced the graduate programme in August 1986. Professor McMahon visited the school in September and stayed with professor C. Byse. In October, professor von Mehren, a colleague and friend of professor Byse, mentioned to me that I was under surveillance, overt and covert. I did not pursue the matter then – the remark was casual; I had only recently arrived in the United States, and over a third of my programme was being taken with professor von Mehren.

9

Nevertheless, I formed the impression that some version of what had transpired in Ireland over the previous eighteen months had been communicated to some faculty members at Harvard.

I was wary. Therefore, when, at the last lecture in December in a course on transnational legal problems with professor Vagts, the latter indicated that he thought one student was likely to fail, I reported this to Andy Kingston, president of the board of student advisors. He thought the statement quoted to be extraordinary and suggested that I discuss it in a subtle way with professor Vagts before the examination took place. This I did. Professor Vagts explained the statement by reference to his concern about an Asian student whose English he considered poor. He may have been referring to a female Asian student on the course who had not at that point been formally admitted to the LL.M. programme – if so, to my own knowledge the student in question had relatively good English and in fact obtained a B+ on her examination course.

Events in the Period January–February, 1987

I was living at 220 Holmes Hall, a room in a Harvard residence within the law school complex. During the first two months of the year, I received a number of anonymous phone calls and what I came to think of later as the 'lights out' treatment. This was unsettling to say the least. For instance, I received a call from a person at 1.30am who refused to identify himself. He asked me if I could refer him to a divorce lawyer, stating that he had received my number in a public house from someone he could not identify. I expressed resentment at the call. Shortly afterwards, the lights, but not the other electrical appliances in the room, went out. The lights came back on after I telephoned facilities the following morning.

On February 27th, I received an early telephone call from Howard Yourow who helped organise talks for the graduate programme. He asked my opinion on professor McMahon with a view to the latter being invited to speak at the Kennedy School of Government. I spoke of professor McMahon's academic abilities, but queried for obvious reasons why he should ask me about him. He then indicated that someone else had invited professor McMahon to speak to the graduate programme on the following March 3rd, and that I might speak with Nancy Porter of the graduate programme staff about that. I immediately telephoned Miss Porter about professor McMahon's schedule. She stated that professor McMahon was teaching at Temple University at the time, and seemed reluctant about my meeting him the following week. Also, she indicated her feeling that professor McMahon would again be visiting the school later in the year.

Later, at breakfast, I met Howard Yourow, who was with a companion, and pressed him on why he should be asking me about McMahon when the administrators of the graduate programme were obviously in contact with him. He was jocose about the matter and apologised for the 'disturbance.' His companion at the time made remarks directed at me about deportation.

Events in the Period March–May, 1987

a. INTRODUCTION

During this period I was subjected to both psychological and physical abuse, as a result of which I was hospitalised twice and in consequence of which I sought representation from a variety of sources and also alternative accommodation. I was to a great extent informed of the process to which I was being subjected by an insider at the school who was well disposed to me and whose name I will not mention at this stage in order to protect him from possible recrimination. Also, I was given a good deal of soft information by a number of people as to what was occurring and also the object of the exercise. It was suggested to me at one stage that three different constituencies had an interest in my progress in the graduate programme.

I will describe the events of this period in terms of what occurred.

b.   What Occurred

(1) Intimations of End Game in Progress and Hostility Expressed:

From early March, intimations were given to me by certain members of the faculty that an End Game was in progress in my regard, the objective of which was to terminate my participation in the graduate programme. It was suggested that, although I might get the necessary credits for the programme, I would not get the degree. A number of faculty members expressed hostility towards my presence at the school, one being more explicit than the others.

(2) *Room Broken Into:*
My room was broken into on March 1, and this was made evident to me. For instance, a dictaphone I had been using (and which I had considered using in order to tape the phone calls) was left switched on and was left clicking at the end of the tape when I arrived back in the room on a Sunday evening.

Confirmation of the break-in was given about a week later in a circular from Rocco Forgione, the dorm officer. The circular indicated that the break-in had been through a window – there was a balcony outside my room, and the latch on my window had been broken.

(3) *Wave of Bad Public Relations:*
In the first week of March, a variety of rumours were spread in my regard, both within the graduate student body and also outside the Law School, for instance, in a public house near the school that I occasionally frequented. These rumours ... suggested that I had 'been thrown out of Ireland.'

These rumours caused me embarrassment in relating to other students in the graduate programme. Also, in the public house referred to, a number of friends made over the previous six months shunned me. One of them, while intoxicated, became highly abusive on one occasion and sought to draw me into a fight. At the time, a friend of mine from Ireland was with me and succeeded in averting a serious incident. I later learned that fighting on the part of a student is a ground for expulsion from the school.

(4) *Anonymous Telephone Calls:*
These continued throughout the period in question and,

during one week in particular, occurred on a daily basis. Often there would be no response when I answered the phone. At other times, the call would be along such lines as 'How is Mr. Bet?,' 'Hello brother, how are you today?,' or 'Is this Jim Godsend?' These phone calls continued during a period of around five weeks when I stayed with relatives in East Cambridge. One of the relatives with whom I stayed had a heart attack, brought about in part, I believe, by the trouble I was in.

(5) *Tapped Phone Lines:*
I believe that my own phone and that of the relatives with whom I stayed in East Cambridge were tapped during the period in question. Apart from the give-away sound that can accompany bugging, I have circumstantial evidence that parties involved in the surveillance had knowledge of my intentions that could only be available through phone tapping. For instance, there was an attempt made to deflect me on my first visit to the Irish consulate in Boston on March 16 after I had made an appointment to call there on my relatives' phone line.

(6) *Surveillance:*
This became blatantly overt for a period of about seven weeks from the beginning of March, and amounted to intimidation and harassment. Around the law school, those conducting the surveillance went out of their way to make their presence evident. In effect, I was let know that I was being 'shadowed.'

The surveillance extended to the dining quarters in the Harkness in the law school and made me so uncomfortable that, for about six weeks, I avoided eating there. It extended to the library, and made concentration difficult and indeed impossible for much of the time.

The surveillance extended to the meetings in a seminar and course taken by me in the Spring term – my performance in theories of firms and markets was scrutinised and criticised by a Denise Madigan, and was scrutinised by a Chuck Kenyon in alternative disputes resolution. Both indicated to me that they were thoroughly familiar with the events of my life over the previous five years and made overtures as to my going to mediation, and to the range of options that would then be available to me. Both persons mentioned were attached to different departments at Harvard University. Denise Madigan was particularly insulting with respect to my contributions to the seminar.

The surveillance extended outside Cambridge. I made several attempts to obtain legal representation and alternative accommodation, and visited Boston, Somerville and Hingham in the processes. Some of these attempts were pointedly frustrated by those carrying out the surveillance. These made their presence known, for instance, by driving with headlights on and hooter blowing behind the taxi in which I might be driving from time to time. Also, individuals approached me on the street and photographed me for no reason.

I had become friendly with a Bill Hayes, a building manager in Cambridge. He was well connected, including in the accommodation field, and was in the habit of helping individuals over from Ireland. He was bemused when all his efforts to find accommodation for me failed.

The surveillance story might be perceived as a manifestation of paranoia. However, it was intimated to me that the End Game is so designed and that the correct classification is 'justified paranoia.' I complained about it on several occasions to the graduate programme administrators and to the general counsel's office of the university and received no denial of the fact of its taking place. Indeed, one of those to whom I complained suggested that I try to stay in New York or Washington for a period and to complete the programme from some such far away place. The overall effect of the surveillance was that I felt hounded and criminalised during the two months or so while it took place.

(7) Literature in Mailbox:
Each of the residents of Holmes Hall had his own mail box. During the period from March to June, I received a flow of

14

unsolicited mail that was calculated to humiliate me and to impel me to leave the school. For instance, literature on emigration and deportation was placed in my box.

(8) Irregularities in Mail:
Between March and June, there were irregularities in my mail deliveries. For instance, ordinary mail from Massachusetts to Ireland normally takes five days. My family noted that some of my letters were taking fifteen days to arrive. A letter sent by me by express post to a relative in Cork took nine days to arrive. Also, I received personal correspondence from the Cayman Islands government representative in London – photocopies rather than originals of his letters were received by me. I sent about four letters to people in Ireland with whom I had been corresponding and never received even an acknowledgement of these letters.

As a result of these irregularities, I arranged that certain of my correspondence be forwarded indirectly by a friend of mine in Boston.

(9) Disruption of Laundry Services:
I had a laundry contract with Harvard Student Agencies, under which my laundry would be deposited on Monday evenings and collected on Thursday evenings. Between March and May this service was disrupted, in the sense that my laundry bags went missing and could not be traced despite numerous requests by me to those involved in the laundry service. Even at the time of my departure from Cambridge in June, one of my laundry bags had still not been found. In order to keep myself in clean clothes, I was obliged to buy new clothes on several occasions during the period in question.

(10) Interference with Atmospherics in Room:
This was by far the most serious complaint I had within the law school during the period from March to June 1987. The interference can properly be characterised only as physical abuse.

The noise complained of generally was a high pitched frequency sound that over a period of time damaged my hearing and has left me with constant earaches.

I first noticed the noise on Sunday evening, March 1, the same evening that I discovered my room to have been broken into. Over a period of about twenty minutes, the high noise level scrambled my brain and traumatised me. The days surrounding March 1 were extraordinary in relation to the residents of the second floor of Holmes Hall in several ways. Another resident of the floor – George Martinex – was hospitalised, having complained of interference with his room, including the defacement of the walls. He subsequently dropped out of the school year. More to the point, two days prior to my hearing the noise on March 1, the occupant of the adjoining room – Phizaisakdi Horayangkara – moved out of his room unexpectedly for a trip to New York, Paris and Thailand. He had not had the money at Christmas to visit his family in Thailand, and his sudden departure was contrary to his plans as he had previously discussed them. The noise I heard on March 1, and subsequently, came from the direction of the adjoining vacant room

I returned to work at the school on March 2, without having discussed the previous evening with anyone apart from relatives. Two residents of the second floor – Louis Perearts (U.S.A.) and Don Arbess (Canada) – were discussing my having 'heard noises in my room the previous night.' One of them approached my door to check whether he could hear the noises.

The shock to me on March 1 was such that over the next six weeks I lived in my room for a period of only one week, and stayed with relatives for most of the remainder of the period.

On April 2, two days after I had returned to my room, after a stay away of a month, the noise re-occurred at about midday and persisted for over an hour. It induced nausea and vertigo, and also caused pains in my heart. I immediately attended the law school clinic, and was seen by Dr. Stampfer, who noted that my critical faculties – blood pres-

16

sure, pulse and temperature – had reached dangerous levels. She arranged for my admission to the Stillman Infirmary immediately.

The third distinct occasion when the noise occurred was on April 12, at about midday. On this occasion the noise persisted for about fifteen minutes and was extremely loud. It caused a severe pain in both my ears, and this pain still persists.

As a result of this pain I was given medication by a Dr. Drake of the Stillman Infirmary, and was also treated by Dr. Kiskaden, an ear specialist at the infirmary. He diagnosed a problem with my hearing, and in particular with my right ear. The noise re-occurred on April 25, and persisted for about three hours. Two other residents of Holmes Hall heard the noise, namely, Bill Markham and Bob Wilkins. This was the first occasion on which I had corroboration of the noise in the room, and I immediately telephoned Harvard Police, who sent a security officer to investigate the complaint. Apart from myself, the other two residents of the hall were available to give statements, but the security officer said that he did not have the authority to take statements.

The effect of the noise has been to impair the hearing in both my ears, and has left me with constant earaches and occasional bouts of dizziness. It has also effected a change in my personality, in part as a result of the trauma involved.

(11) Medical Malpractice and Theft in the Stillman Infirmary: I was admitted to the Stillman Infirmary of the university on April 2 because of the effect of the noise levels on my critical faculties. I slept there for about six nights, but, for the reasons given below, sought otherwise to avoid the infirmary as much as possible. I was admitted to room 501.

I was attended that evening by Dr. Hewitt of the law school clinic. After I told him about the noise in the room, he said that he expected the scheduled tests to show nothing, and I was suffering from 'what we call nausea and vertigo.' He prescribed a pure liquid diet for me.

17

The following days, without my consent, I was attended by Dr. Cooley of the Harvard Medical School. I protested and he said that Dr. Hewitt was unavailable – I was told by nurses that Dr. Hewitt was in the infirmary every day. Dr Cooley tried to make me feel like a prisoner in the infirmary – 'Does Mr. Linehan have the privilege of going out?'

I protested against the starvation diet, and was forced to leave the infirmary during the day if for no other reason than to eat properly.

Dr. Cooley asked me if I would make a deal with him – he said that things generally could be sorted out if I stayed in the Infirmary for a week. I refused to make a deal and he dropped out of the picture after he admitted that 'most of my mistakes are walking around.'

Then, without my consent, I was attended by Dr. Carpe of the law school clinic. She tried to make out that ... I was unhappy because I was 35! She asked me if I was behind in my studies – I told her I was a month ahead on these. She tried to discourage me from continuing my studies. Without my telling her, Dr. Carpe mentioned the 'poison pill' and 'green mail' treatment I got at prof. Sanders lecture on April 7. This is elaborated on elsewhere. Suffice to say here that, without my knowledge or consent, I was given a sedative when I was leaving the Infirmary in order to go to that lecture.

My experience in the infirmary was a travesty of all that medicine is about. Apart from the foregoing, I never saw the same nurse more than twice. The bed I was in was an automatic one, and its position was adjusted differently every night so that I was forced to try to sleep in different uncomfortable positions. The bed was changed literally once during my few days in the infirmary. I protested to a nurse about this, and was told that they changed the bed daily as a matter of practice!

There were two beds in room 501. In order to reach my own, I had to pass the other bed. This was set up with a large orthopaedic device that extended across the passage-

way. This device was lowered regularly so that I had to bend down in order to pass through to my own bed.

On April 9, when I stopped sleeping in the infirmary, I discovered that personal notes had been taken from my inside coat pocket and reported this at the infirmary and at the graduate office.

There is no doubt in my mind that room 501 was designed as a type of 'nut cracker suite' and that the treatment given me there was part of the End Game. One of the nurses – who had come originally from Ireland about thirty years ago – confirmed this. She advised me to pack it up, and that it was never worth it to fight them.

(12) *Statements of Hostility from the Faculty:*
I took two courses with professor Von Mehren, and he also supervised my thesis. In the Fall, as already mentioned, he told me that I was under overt and covert surveillance and, about the same time, admitted that he had heard about the circumstances in which I had left U.C.C.

On March 13, after the surveillance had become manifest, after my room had been broken into, after I had been traumatised by the noise levels in my room, and after a toilet roll had been left in my carrel, I returned to professor Von Mehren and stated some of these complaints to him, and asked if I had questions to answer. He said that I had no questions to answer, but that hostility had arisen in my regard.

On March 16, I met professor Vagts and he asked me if I 'was ready to wrap it up.' He became evasive when I asked him what he meant.

Around the same time, when receiving a copy of my Fall and Winter grades from Nancy Porter in the graduate office, she intimated in a subtle way that although I might get the grades I might not get the degree.

On April 7, together with the graduate student representative and two other graduate students, I complained to professor Snyder, dean of the graduate programme, about my room, the surveillance, posters that had been left on or about the vicinity of my room and about the toilet roll that had been left in my carrel. The students who accompanied me were Fabrizio Arossa (Italy), Manuel Caceres (Paraguay) and Alfredo Conseco (Peru). Professor Snyder's initial response was mocking – he asked me if 'I'd had enough.' Subsequently, as is later discussed, he gave the semblance of being helpful.

On April 8, I went to professor Von Mehren's office. He approved my thesis in a grudging manner, and his closing remark (it being raining heavily that day) was that 'maybe the weather will change and you won't feel so much at home here.'

On the same day, I met coincidentally with professor Vagts. Completely out of the blue, he started talking about grass! He said that most of the grass in New England was green but that sometimes it got mixed up with the short stubble brown grass found down South. In New England, he said, they made every effort to dig out the brown grass. In response to this apparently lunatic comment, I remarked that the brown grass was a sturdy growth.

Apart from the foregoing, between March and May, I got strong intimations from professor Sander (with whom I was taking a Spring course) that my dropping out of the programme would have been welcome. professor Kraakman, a visiting professor from Yale, with whom I was taking a second Spring course, intimated also that there was an End Game in progress

(13) *Poison Pill and Green Mail:*
On April 7 and 8, I was administered the 'Poison Pill' treatment previously referred to. When leaving the Stillman Infirmary to attend a lecture by professor Sanders, I was given medicine that I shortly discovered to be a sedative. On arrival at the classroom, there was an apparently gratuitous notice on the black-board that read "case normally worth a settlement of $15,000 to $150,000. I settle for $50,000."

There was a small number at the lecture, and several left during the course of it because of its (to them) apparent irrelevancy and meandering. Professor Sander introduced

20

as a speaker a Tom Bishop who practices as a lawyer/mediator, and the latter proceeded to talk about 'divorce and mediation.' ... There was a reference to the coercive aspect of mediation, and how 'a person might come home from the office one day and find his child missing.'

The entire presentation was totally unexpected by me, and opened old wounds and created fears to such an extent that I had to leave for part of the lecture. Chuck Kenyon, previously mentioned, followed me to the bathroom. During the lecture, it was indicated that the Legal Services Corporation in Boston was available to those who wished mediation.

The poison pill at this lecture seemed like the final straw, and it took me five hours after the lecture in my room to recover any sort of composure. I then returned to the Stillman Infirmary. My bed had again been changed, and I complained over the intercom. The response given to me was by way of a question – 'Had I had enough?' I told her I was going to the Legal Services Corporation for representation. She had pre-knowledge about the presentation at the previous day's lecture – she drew it up and tried to emphasise that it was about divorce. I insisted that I was going for representation. She questioned me as to whether I was trying to find out 'How corporate America worked,' and I answered her 'Something like that.'

From a telephone directory I discovered that Legal Services Corporation was at 84 State Street, Boston, telephone 223-0230. I was directed to the top floor of the skyscraper involved. There were two people in the office I was referred to. They were sheepish about their functions, but said that they did not provide legal services.

A secretary in another part of the building telephoned about the number of the Legal Services Corporation. She was told that it was a government number and that it had been disconnected. She said that she did not understand it at all.

At another such lecture in professor Sanders' course, on April 28, after what was described as 'flag-waving' in my direction, I introduced myself to David O'Connor of the

Massachusetts Mediation Service. He referred me to Till-inghast, Collins and Graham as experienced settlement lawyers.

(14) Poster Campaign:

During March and April, a series of posters was placed about the vicinity of my room at Holmes Hall – for instance, on the two hall doors leading to my room and on the door of the bathroom used by me. Taken with what else was going on, these had a constant unsettling and intimidatory effect.

These posters included captions such as 'Grades are Random,' 'Are Grades a Burning Issue?' (I was one of the few smokers on the second floor of Holmes Hall). 'I've been down so long, this feels like up,' 'Wing it' and 'Life after Law School looks so bright I gotta wear shades.'

Other residents found these posters 'distasteful' and one of the resident assistants complained to the Dean of Students office, without avail. I understood the posters to be directed at me. This was confirmed when a poster was placed overnight on the bathroom door I used on April 14, advertising an anti-CIA rally in Washington on the following April 25-27. It contained a stamped notice 'Phone Boston 423-0028. Interpreted for the Hearing Impaired.'

My hearing had been impaired and I phoned the number for 'an interpretation.' My identity was known to the person who answered the phone and I was strongly urged to go on the trip. Expenses would be paid. Most of the group going would stay in Washington on Saturday and Sunday (and it was put to me that I would wish to return repeatedly). On the Monday, I would attend a protest outside CIA headquarters in Virginia. 'Some people would be arrested during the protest.' To arrange the trip, I was given the name of an individual at Harvard, a Debbie Satz, who was attached to the social studies department.

I discussed it with a friend at Holmes Hall who knew what was happening generally. His advice was not to go – 'There would be a lot of people in Washington and Virginia. Anything could happen.' I phoned Debbie Satz and declined the invitation.

(15) *Lights Out Treatment:*

Brief reference has already been made to the 'Lights Out' treatment I received occasionally in January and February. This usually occurred shortly after I would have received an anonymous phone call.

The 'Lights Out' treatment intensified in April and May, and re-occurred once in June. It extended to the lights in the corridor leading from the hall door to my room corridor, this corridor being illuminated directly by three long fluorescent lights and indirectly by one such light.

In the space of three weeks in April, for instance, three of the four lights in the corridor were switched off at different times and left unattended for extended periods despite complaints by other residents, and by the resident assistant of the second floor. The lights were switched off at one period in such a way that the corridor leading from the hall door to my room was in total darkness, while the remainder of the corridor was lighted.

Other residents appreciated the symbolism, namely, that my continuing status as a student was problematical for the university. Some of these residents were friends of mine, and pulled the fuse wires out of the lights so that they were left hanging down reaching half-way to the floor. The light problem seemed to have been dealt with by April 20th.

On the evening of April 25, I obtained corroboration by two other residents of the interference with the atmospherics in my room, and was therefore in a position to phone Harvard police, which I did. During the following night, the light directly outside my room was switched off, and left in that condition despite my complaint to facilities. It was lighted again only after I complained to the general counsel's office of the university on the basis that I would revert to the Irish consulate unless the physical and psychological abuse was stopped.

In the third week of May, after I had nearly died from shock in intensive care in The Malden Hospital, and after I had finished the degree programme, the Dean of the graduate office and of student affairs suggested that I go home immediately – to obtain medical treatment and (per Dean Snyder) before I start writing the thing up. I intended doing that, and also wished to stay for commencement on June 11.

However, on the evening of May 28, the lights on the corridor were switched off again. At the same time the desk and ceiling lights in my room were switched on and off alternately for a period of about half-an-hour. I had corroboration of this, since a friend of mine from Ireland was in the room, and was therefore again in a position to phone facilities without being open to the accusation of 'imagining things' or worse. The lights were switched on again quickly. However, for the rest of the evening I was fending off a panic attack such as had landed me in The Malden Hospital.

I phoned the Irish consulate the following morning and updated the consul, Mr. Patrick Curran. He had been in touch with the Irish department of foreign affairs in Dublin about the affair and, at that point, led me to understand that he would make a direct representation to the general counsel's office of the university. He also advised me to go home as quickly as possible.

(16) Various:

Apart from the foregoing, during the period in question, I was subjected to intimidation in a variety of forms, for instance through mimicry and symbolism.

Moreover, in the course of attempts to obtain alternative accommodation and legal representation, I was subjected to a number of very frightening incidents. For instance, on April 6, while seeking assistance at the international institute in Boston, a phone call was made to the receptionist, who was attending me, telling her not to help me.

Also, I was taken for what might be described as 'joy rides' in cabs on two occasions in the course of my trips to Boston, Somerville and Hingham. Corroboration of an attempt to bring me on another such trip is available.

On April 5, there were suspicious circumstances sur-

24

rounding a cab that came to collect me on the evening of my visit to Glastonbury Abbey in Hingham. James Lagropperia, the business manager at the abbey, also became suspicious and questioned the cab driver who arrived to pick me up. He suggested that I might be safer to travel back to Cambridge by public transport, and drove me to Quincy for that purpose.

Within the university, I got what might be termed the 'run around' from certain members of the staff. For instance, on April 7, as already mentioned, I went to Dean Snyder with a delegation including the LL.M. representative and two other graduate students. I complained about the problems in my room, in the library and also about the surveillance. In the presence of the delegation, Dean Snyder phoned the dorm officer and offered me the choice of three double suites within the law school accommodation. I went to the dorm officer on the following day and he said that he was not assigning any of the suites in question to me. I again asked Dean Snyder to attempt to get bed and breakfast accommodation for me in Cambridge or some adjoining place for the duration of the LL.M. programme. Through J.P. O'Connor of the graduate office staff, I was informed that no such accommodation seemed to be available. Moreover, he remarked to me that Dean Snyder said to mention that if I were to get alternative accommodation 'I would only be going out of the frying pan and into the fire!'

I was left with no option but to return to the dorm room in Holmes Hall. On April 9, the lock was changed in the room as a condition of my moving back there. The person who changed the lock warned me that I was in danger of psychological damage and that he hadn't seen a case like this since the 1950's. He left one key instead of two (one for the hall door and one for the room door). This key did not open the room door, and I found myself shut out of my room. I went to the dorm officer, who was abusive. He referred me to another part of the university in order to collect the correct keys, and gave me the name of a person to ask for. The *person named was 'on vacation' and I was referred else-where for keys.*

Another incident stands out. In May, an acquaintance went out of his way to hand me a pamphlet with the unlike-ly title of 'Veritas Revisited,' Veritas being the university logo. The pamphlet contained a number of articles that made a parody of scripture, and also contained a two column story about an individual who had been involved in a number of disputes over a three year period. This indi-vidual had one son whose skull was fractured at a swim-ming pool. I asked the carrier of the pamphlet about it – he said that 'everyone' had received one in their mailbox. Enquiries about this proved the statement a lie.

The period from February to June was a long one in which a great deal occurred.

The foregoing is only a partial summary. The entire experience was terrifying and seemed clearly designed to de-stabilise me. It involved the disruption of my living, working and social environments combined with the with-drawal of supportive agencies within and outside the uni-versity that one would in the normal course of events expect to be of assistance.

...

Conclusion

It is clear to me who the three constituencies interested in my progress in the graduate programme were. Basically, however, I fell foul of a fluent End Game based on notions of gatekeepers liability and was designated to be one of the 1% of Harvard's attrition rate.

My hearing is impaired. I am not qualified to assess the psy-chological damage.

Aer Lingus, when made aware of my condition, agreed to fly me home only under certain conditions.

The foregoing deposition was sworn before a peace com-missioner on August 31, 1987. The type of sonic device referred to in it has been in use for decades by security forces. Certain of these devices emit a hard, physical, staccato noise. It could remind one of a hard-beaked bird tapping on a tree trunk. For that reason, its given code name is *Woodpecker*.

2 Weight of the Evidence

In May, 1987, I was seriously injured at Harvard. That central fact was expressed in a very muted manner in the Irish High Court judgment of January 31, 1992, that was appealed to the Irish Supreme Court.

It correctly recited that:-

"Physically the Applicant has become grossly overweight and had difficulties on his return to Cork in 1987 in getting around."

Although the abuse at Harvard was appalling, the techniques used and described in the deposition of August 31, 1987, are standard in certain circles. Some of them were at issue in the *Case of Ireland v. The United Kingdom* (a judgment of the European Court of Human Rights of January 18, 1978). Part of a report of that judgment reads:-

"The court took formal note of that undertaking. However, it held unanimously that, although certain violations of Article 3 were not contested, a ruling should nevertheless be given thereon. It appraised the situation in the various interrogation or detention centres.

First Case: unidentified centre or centres. In August and October 1971, fourteen persons had been detained at an unidentified centre or centres and submitted to a form of 'interrogation in depth.' This had involved the combined application of 'five techniques' which consisted basically of hooding the detainees, subjecting them to a continuous loud hissing noise, depriving them of sleep, subjecting them to a reduced diet and making them stand for periods of some hours against a wall in a painful posture. Detailed evidence regarding two such persons revealed that the 'disorientation' and 'sensory deprivation' techniques, as they were sometimes termed, had been applied to them, with intermittent periods of respite of undetermined length, during four or possibly five days. The court noted that the techniques had been applied in combination, with premeditation and for hours at a stretch, and had caused, if not actual bodily injury, at least intense physical and mental suffering and had led to acute psychiatric disturbances during interrogation. They had been such as to arouse in their victims feelings of fear, anguish and inferiority capable of humiliating and debasing them and possibly breaking their physical or moral resistance.

The court held, by sixteen votes to one, that the use of the five techniques constitutes a practice of inhuman or degrading treatment."

The treatment of me at Harvard in 1987 was worse and more extended than described. Although startling, it is not altogether surprising. Harvard and similar institutions develop such techniques as part of ongoing research, and it might seem almost reasonable to their administrators to use them in effecting attrition policies. The alternative of writing a letter to the effect that *"We've changed our minds about you. Please pack your belongings and leave"* would undoubtedly involve Harvard in a continuous stream of million dollar litigation from irate students, with ready-made proofs for the breach of contracts cases. That would be an unattractive option in an environment dominated by the dollar factor.

As indicated by my deposition of August 31, 1987, the *Good Night Saigon* routine used against me at Harvard in 1987 seemed to be endemic in Harvard's administration. It was apparently used as a cost-saving attrition routine to force out students, for whatever reason, without payment of compensation.

Prior to the High Court settlement dated July 9, 1986, I had been required to undergo a medical examination with Dr. T. O'Connell, a physician nominated by U.C.C. His report represented me as having been in good physical health in June 1986.

The next extensive medical reports on my health date from May 10 and 11, 1987. At that time, I was confined to intensive care at The Malden Hospital, Massachusetts, with a suspected heart attack and other injuries. That confinement marked the onset of partial invalidity that has continued in the meantime. My life was in the balance for two days at the time, and I was attended by about ten medical personnel, all but one of whom were independent of Harvard university.

The Malden reports do more than record the onset of physical disability. They record the immediate causes - Dr. O'Leary's notes stated in relation to me:-

"Speaks of the 'end game' at the law school, and states that the atmospherics in his room have been altered."

Similarly, Dr. Olan's notes state that:-

"The patient stated that he was a Harvard Law Student and was deemed persecuted by an old law professor. He stated that he 'wasn't crazy' and 'they were trying to get him by putting microphones in his dorm room'."

At that time, my life was in the balance. Accordingly, it was submitted in the appeal to the Supreme Court that the contemporaneous independent medical reports had a credibility status not unlike that of a death bed confession.

The nature and causes of the invalidity were noted in reports of Dr. C. Kenefick to Joseph Cuddigan, solicitor, of July and August 1987. In his report dated August 20, Dr. Kenefick noted:-

"In reply to your letter dated 13th inst., for Mr. Linehan to acquire severe hearing loss in one ear of the degree that he has in his right ear would in my opinion, require noise of great intensity for it to come on suddenly"

Joseph Cuddigan's testimony in the High Court also

clearly dated my invalidity from events in Harvard in 1987.

"I know that after Mr. Linehan came back from his sabbatical in Harvard, his health appeared to me to be very bad, My Lord. He was grossly overweight and from what documents were in existence from Harvard, it appeared that he had some major health problems in America and from that period his health on occasions would appear to be quite bad, My Lord."

Mr. Cuddigan had been contacted by me between March and May, 1987. After I returned from Harvard in June, 1987, he had acted in the compensation case against Harvard as well as in the pension case against U.C.C. He testified as to his instructions at that period:-

"That is correct, my Lord, Mr. Linehan instructed me that while he was at Harvard he was subjected to various forms of electronic and other types of harassment and on his behalf I wrote to a firm of lawyers in America furnishing them with a statement of what I had been told had happened. In addition, there were photocopied medical reports from a hospital in America."

The electronic harassment referred to by Mr. Cuddigan was in fact severe abuse with a sonic device for a number of hours at irregular periods over a number of months. The type of device used has been litigated in England in *R. v. Laming*. In presenting the case, the submissions of Mr. Goldberg, Q.C., were in part as follows:-

"It is equivalent in suddenness to the horse to a loud firework exploding in its ear, although the actual noise would be more equivalent in human terms to a hideous ear-piercing shriek best compared to the noise of a very loud <u>microphone</u> that has gone wrong. The effect on a horse was to put it off stride completely and often to throw the jockey, which meant that the race was lost …

It could be focused like a torch 'right into the horses ears as it gallops past" with a force of more than 22 watts.
IT LEFT NO EVIDENCE OF ITS USE … [Emphasis added].

Thus James Laming had invented the perfect way of nob-

bling racehorses."

The word "microphone" in Mr. Goldberg's submission has been underlined. That is precisely the word used by me as quoted in The Malden Hospital notes of May 10 and 11, 1987, when my life was in the balance over two days.

The onset of partial invalidity from May, 1987, was also noted in the testimony of Mrs. P. O'Connell. That invalidity manifested itself in obesity, by reason of my physical dysfunctioning.

Appellant
"Did I ever have a weight problem, Mrs. O'Connell?"
Mrs. O'Connell
"You did."
Appellant
"When?"
Mrs. O'Connell
"When you came back from America I seen a terrible change in you."
Appellant
"In what way?"
Mrs. O'Connell
"You kind of bloated up with it."
Appellant
"In the meantime, since 1987, have I been a very active person?"
Mrs. O'Connell
"Not to my knowledge."
Appellant
"Was I an active person before 1987?"
Mrs. O'Connell
"You were always."

Because of increasing physical dysfunctioning, I had required home nursing assistance since 1989. I employed Nurse Clear in that capacity in 1990. Her testimony in the High Court identified the true nature of the dysfunctioning.

"I observed Mr. Linehan to be very overweight and he

appeared to have difficulty caring for himself. He appeared to drag his heels when walking. He appeared to lack muscle tone in his hands and I observed the clumsiness that he would complain about; he was easily stressed and there was an element of post-traumatic stress disorder after all the terrible time he had been through."

By the time of the High Court hearing, Nurse Clear had known me on a day-in-day-out basis for more than two years. She refuted all the suggestions sought to be insinuated by the illegally obtained defamatory report of Dr. Murphy, who had met me for about forty minutes in October 1989.

Appellant

"Exactly. Am I a person who would imagine something that doesn't exist?"

Nurse Clear

"No, I have seen no evidence of delusionary behaviour, thoughts or anything like that." "

As will be seen, one complaint against the High Court hearing is that evidence by way of testimony of both the invalidity, and the causes thereof, was largely excluded. In addition, the judgment appealed against virtually ignored that evidence.

3 Cover-Up Plan

The problem for university administrators in May, 1987, was that I had suffered serious personal injuries of a permanent nature as a result of retaliatory abuse. An abundance of independent proof, including medical evidence, existed.

The cover-up solution quickly gelled as the obvious solution to the *May, 1987, problem* in the minds of the administrations concerned. The scenarios that have unfolded since that month prove that conclusively.

The appeal to the Irish Supreme Court, in the consequential pension case against University College Cork, involved only a claim to a small pension of about £125 net a week in respect of incapacity arising during employment with that university. In the High Court, I put it that the entire defence to a pension claim since 1987 had been farcical, and that relevant law had been totally ignored. Furthermore, it was contended that the evidence established serious illegality practised against me on foot of a cover-up since 1987.

The conduct in question had become an issue in the pension case by reason of University College Cork - and Harvard - having used the pension case since 1987 to forestall the personal injuries litigation and to discredit me.

The extensive *dramatis personae* referred to in the appeal to the Irish Supreme Court reflected partly the fact that the abuses within University College Cork and Harvard in the 1985-1987 period occurred under the authorisation of senior administrators.

The actions of the university affiliated personnel over the period in question requires to be assessed in term of what is, namely, the subtle manifestation of sophisticated, calculating academic minds. Furthermore many of the main protagonists were experienced and highly qualified lawyers. Some bore a long-standing animosity for me. For these reasons, the facts of the case were extensive and complex. Since May, 1987, moreover, limitless financial resources were available to effect a cover-up. Also, the know-how of the two universities involved had been brought to bear in order to screen the background to my confinement in intensive care at The Malden Hospital in May, 1987.

On April 22, 1988, Charles Haughey, then Irish prime minister, met senior administrators at Harvard. The meeting puzzled both expert and casual observers alike. Haughey's U.S. visit was covered by Stephen Collins, political correspondent. In the Sunday Press, on April 24, 1988,

Collins wrote that:-

> *"... Mr. Haughey has taken the unusual step of spending the last two days of his U.S. visit at the Kennedy home as well as delivering a lecture at Harvard, sponsored by the Kennedy School of Government at the famous university."*

The fact that Haughey's talk at Harvard was sponsored by the university indicates a financial arrangement. After the lecture, Haughey consorted with Harvard administrators. Máire Crowe, in the Sunday Tribune on April 24, 1988, reported on the sequence as follows:-

> *"... That session over, he paused for tea and briefings, before being whisked to the next date ... 'Hey, so what's going down, man?' a Harvard student asked. 'Gee, I don't know. I don't know what it's all about,' her acquaintance foggily replied."*

Haughey's unusual meeting with Harvard administrators in April, 1988, caused me disquiet even then. My suspicions were fuelled thereafter as the evidence mounted of involvement by state personnel in the university cover-up attempts after 1987. These suspicions were confirmed when a close associate of Haughey purported to reverse a Supreme Court costs order against U.C.C., with Harvard, in 1993.

Evidence given to the payments to politicians tribunal in 1997 added a new dimension to the speculation as to what deal may have been done between Harvard, U.C.C. and Haughey for political support for a cover-up. That tribunal heard evidence that Haughey had serious financial difficulties in 1987 and thereafter, and that a number of wealthy sources were being approached in an effort to raise a sum in the region of £1 million to help him.

From 1987, I became the subject of a smear campaign. Dr. Murphy's report of October 3, 1989, encapsulated the concocted notions that had by then been directed at me.

In order to put that report, and indeed testimony of Dr. Dineen in the High Court in context, it is necessary to refer briefly to the branch of hostilities known as psychopolitics. Following is a brief excerpt from a Manual of Instructions of Psychopolitical Warfare, by K. Goff, that was relevant to the pension case by putting the interventions of the aforesaid doctors in proper context:

'When the loyalty of an individual cannot be secured, and where the opinion , weight, or effectiveness of the individual stands in the way of [our] goals, it is usually best to occasion a mild neurosis in the person by any available means, and then having carefully given him a history of mental imbalance, to see to it that he disposes of himself in such a way as to resemble suicide. Psychopolitical operators have handled such situations skillfully tens of thousands of times....

One of the first and foremost missions of the psychopolitician is to make an attack upon (us) and insanity synonymous. It should become a definition of insanity, of the paranoid variety, that "a paranoid believes he is being attacked by (us)." Thus, at once, the support of the individual so attacking (us), will fall away and wither.

The cleverness of our attack in this field of Psychopolitics is adequate to avoid the understanding of the layman and the usual stupid official, and by operating entirely under the banner of authority with the oft-repeated statement that the principles of psychotherapy are too devious for common understanding, an entire revolution can be effected without the suspicion of a populace until it is an accomplished fact.

As insanity is the maximum misalignment, it can be grasped to be the maximum weapon."

Although my health was then virtually destroyed, in the meantime, until my success in the Irish Supreme Court in July, 1992, the only money paid to me by either university was £52.25 in respect of travelling expenses in 1989 to meet Dr. Murphy in what transpired to be an illegal premeditated *sheep-dipping* operation. The High Court judgment of January 31, 1992, had passed over several proven episodes of serious illegality by university interests in 1989 after notice of High Court proceedings was given. Perversely, it adverted uncritically to the second tier of defamatory medical evidence then concocted by those episodes.

4 Appeal to Irish Supreme Court

It was submitted to the Irish Supreme Court that a proper scrutiny of relevant facts and law established that I was entitled to a Statute 79 pension from July, 1987. It was also submitted that a proper scrutiny of the conduct of University College Cork's finance committee, acting as its pension committee, between 1987 and 1989, established wholesale infringement of the principles of natural and constitutional justice expressly pleaded in the case by reference to the numerous standard authorities on that subject. The reason for these breaches of natural and constitutional justice was not, it was submitted, ignorance of same. Rather, the primary concern of the university administrators, after the *May, 1987, problem* had occurred, was to cover-up. That entailed a wall of silence.

It was contended that the aforesaid submissions had not been accepted by the High Court, not because of their invalidity or incorrectness, but rather because the evidence before the court established or tended to establish a further accumulation of serious deliberate wrongdoing by U.C.C. administrators in the 1987 to 1989 period. The hearing of the pension case might reasonably have been expected to take place in early 1988 in Cork District Court. Instead, principally by reason of delaying tactics on behalf of U.C.C. and Harvard, it did not take place until October and December, 1991, in the High Court. In consequence, the High Court was confronted in 1991 with a mass of evidence that proved or tended to prove the very serious wrongdoing on foot of a cover-up that had taken place in the interim since 1987. In that interim, resort to delaying tactics was one of the major strategies of the universities, to the intent of putting as much time as possible between events in the 1985-1987 period and the hearing of resulting litigation. It was put that high level expertise from both universities had been brought to bear in implementing that strategy, and that it had been done successfully.

The pension case on appeal was but one of two distinct cases arising from the facts herein. The major case, that is the matrix of two of the others, was in respect of personal injuries sustained at Harvard university in 1987. The damages claimed in that case have been reasonably estimated at $10 million.

Only the pension case was pleaded and at issue in the High Court in the proceedings arising from which the appeal to the Irish Supreme Court was based. However, the presiding judge was apprised of the other cases during the hearing.

5 Manoeuvres Prior to the High Court

A major damage-limitation exercise began in the litigation complex after May, 1987, and continued – as will be seen – up to, during, and beyond the High Court hearing in the pension case. Manipulation was the name of the game. Evidence, parties, and witnesses would be manipulated on a free style basis to the desired objective of finality.

The following is a brief and incomplete survey of the manipulations that occurred between May, 1987, and the commencement of the High Court hearing in October, 1991. First, Aer Lingus refused to carry me from Boston to Shannon in June, 1987, without medical assurances. Harvard furnished a letter dated June 4, 1987, from Dr. Reid, a psychiatrist, with obvious intended insinuation. In some respects this letter may be seen as the beginning of the smear campaign.

Secondly, Michael Keating, Harvard nominated mediator, promised vigorous representation in 1987 for compensation, but departed the scene in 1988 after the pension case had progressed in Cork District Court. Thirdly, U.C.C.'s finance committee, acting as its pension committee, gave a cursory refusal of my pension claim in 1987. That committee was controlled by the same individuals who had engineered relevant events in the period 1985 to 1987.

Fourthly, vigorous attempts to arrange a hearing of the pension case in Cork District Court in 1987 and 1988 were avoided by the simple expedient of key witnesses circumventing witness summonses. Fifthly, parties complicit in, present at, or knowledgeable of relevant events in the period 1985-1986 departed U.C.C. by way of early retirement. Sixthly, after High Court proceedings were notified in March, 1989, these were delayed for a year through a bogus solicitation of a further unnecessary pension application. Blatant fraud was resorted to as a plausible basis for this exercise.

Seventhly, the 1989 exercise took a callous and serious illegal turn, between July and October, 1989. In that period, through irregular interventions by U.C.C. medical affiliates, I was *sheep-dipped*. The object of the hit-and-run approaches was indicated by Dr. Murphy's report of October 3, 1989. Faced with High Court proceedings, the financial controllers of U.C.C. and Harvard had immediately developed a cadre of "professional" witnesses. Eighthly, High Court orders for judicial review and discovery were obtained on my behalf in early 1990. The former was responded to by a bland statement of opposition and replying affidavit. Ninthly, some six interlocutory applications were necessitated to obtain a partial compliance with the discovery order, between July and November, 1990.

Tenthly, by late November, 1990, a date for hearing of

the review was provisionally set for early February, 1991. At that stage, a mass of documentation was released for inspection. A substantial part of the documentation was irrelevant, and most was jumbled in such a way as to conceal sequences of events.

Between February and July, 1991, I put extensive evidence on record through affidavits and exhibits. At that stage, U.C.C. successfully applied for an oral hearing in which the documentary evidence would be circumvented. Notwithstanding this application, the university called no witnesses to the eventual hearing in October and December, 1991. Eleventhly, between August and September, 1991, I issued over fifty subpoena, several of which by necessity were in respect of witnesses that were likely to be adverse or hostile. Without such subpoena, most of these witnesses would undoubtedly not have appeared.

Twelfthly, persons serving these subpoena were in some cases met with outright hostility. Aidan Moran, U.C.C. registrar, forbade the service of subpoena within U.C.C.

Thirteenthly, throughout the 1987-1991 period, U.C.C. agents refused to refer in any form to Harvard. I knew that continuous liaison had taken place between senior administrators of the two universities from 1986 onwards, in the aftermath of the 1986 High Court case, and that agents, legal and other, had been briefed accordingly. Fourteenthly, in the weeks prior to the commencement of the hearing in October, 1991, questionable and questioned medical certificates were furnished to excuse the attendance of the late Tadhg O'Ciardha, former U.C.C. president, and Francis Jacob, former U.C.C. treasurer. Thus, at the eleventh hour, two of the principal background manipulators circumvented the subpoena served on them.

Fifteenthly, although he was a principal witness, no reply was received in respect of a subpoena served on Bryan McMahon, solicitor. This was a repeat performance by him. He had also failed to respond to a witness summons for him served on U.C.C. in 1988. He was aware of the case that was being made.

As will be seen, it was contended on appeal that the High Court hearing was deficient in many respects in the basic essentials of justice. However, the two facets of, first, the absence of key witnesses and secondly, the use of fabricated medical evidence, meant that the hearing could be at best a cosmetic and misleading exercise unless authentic first-hand documentary evidence was relied on.

6 *Manipulations During High Court Hearing*

Notwithstanding that it called no witnesses, a critical assessment of the transcript of testimony in the High Court reveals a definite scheme by U.C.C. for manipulating the eventual format of the presentation to the court. Three specific objectives can be identified:- first, the imposition of a smear on me by means of fabricated evidence; secondly, the maintenance of the *wall of silence* that had been erected after I was admitted to intensive care in Malden Hospital in May, 1987; and thirdly, a particularly studied by-pass of specific issues such as the liaison with Harvard university, and the illegal fabrication of medical evidence in 1989.

U.C.C. pointedly disrupted my schedule of witnesses at the commencement of the hearing in October, 1991, and again at the re-commencement of the hearing in December, 1991. On both occasions, this disruption had the effect of bringing forward witnesses who would seek to impose a false and fabricated psychological smear on me and thus pollute the evidence.

It was contended in the appeal, and in other proceedings, that I had been subjected to a *sheep-dipping* exercise in 1989 after notice of High Court proceedings was given, in the course of which defamatory evidence was illegally fabricated. It was also contended that the circumstances of that fabrication constituted a callous violation of my rights under the European Convention.

One obvious legacy from that period was Dr. Murphy's report of October 3, 1989. U.C.C. relied on it in the hearing. Justice Barron expressly ruled the report as irrelevant. Anomalously, he subsequently adopted it in the judgment.

Throughout the hearing, U.C.C. administrators affected general amnesia on virtually all material facts. That pattern was glaring.

Subpoena had been served on witnesses summoned to the hearing. Most university administrators ignored the requirement of these subpoenas to bring relevant documentation, with the obvious effect of prolonging the hearing and taking from their testimony. That pattern was also glaring.

Certain witnesses served with subpoena simply refused, without any basis being tendered either to me or to the High Court, to attend the court. Bryan McMahon, a key witness, did not attend court. The late Tadhg O'Ciardha, another key witness, also did not attend court.

Having applied for an oral hearing in July 1991, and thereby virtually circumventing affidavits and exhibits properly admitted in evidence over the previous sixteen months, U.C.C. called no witnesses.

A clear pattern is also evident throughout the transcript of university administrators avoiding questions by evasive answers. A notable example is provided in an answer by Michael Mortell, that made no reference to legal advice furnished from Harvard university since 1987:

Justice Barron
"Who do you receive advice from?"
M. Mortell
"From the Secretary of the College, M. Kelleher and if needs be legal advice, and for anything along those lines we would have that kind of advice. I would bend my mind to that problem at that time, because it wasn't within my direct admin-

istrative function. I would then go back and do my own busi-
ness and I wouldn't carry the details around in my mind at
the time. I would discuss the question, we would have the
advice with the statutes, saying what interpretations that
you .... legal advice and so on, and then on that basis we would
make a recommendation. Now, that is not to say that I should
consider the rest of my life carrying those sort of details in
my mind. Now, if I were the Secretary of the college I cer-
tainly would or if they were things that impinged directly on
me in my administrative function where I will need to know
the details and carry them with me, I certainly would, but
this was not an area for which I had prime responsibility. I
hope, My Lord, I have made clear what the process ...."
Mr. Justice Barron
"Yes." "

In conclusion, one can summarise that university
administrators were substantially successful in maintaining the *wall of silence* erected after the abuse and injuries
inflicted at Harvard in 1987. This was achieved in significant part by a distinct policy of non-cooperation at the
High Court hearing.

University witnesses repeatedly resorted to downright
pantomime in side-stepping the Harvard dimension. The
following are five examples of disingenuous responses in
so doing. First, when asked about my confinement in
intensive care in May, 1987, Michael Mortell, U.C.C. president, pretended not to know of same.

Appellant
"Still on the question of medical evidence, you were pre-
sumably at this point aware that in 1987 I was admitted in
intensive care in a hospital in America?"
Mr. Mortell
"In where?"
Appellant
"In America."
Mr. Mortell

"I sat at the back before lunch and I heard you mention that you had been in Intensive Care. I didn't know that and I certainly didn't know where."

There is a clear inconsistency between those answers and Mortell's following testimony:-

Appellant

"Did I understand you, professor, to say that you hadn't seen those documents previously?"

Mr. Mortell

"No, you asked me did I recollect seeing them and I said no. But I did make the overall comment that the Committee is very well briefed and my clear recollection is that we knew we had a difficult case on our hands and would have been particularly well briefed."

Secondly, Cyril Deasy, deputy finance officer, U.C.C., swore an affidavit dated July 22, 1991, whereby he acknowledged the *considerable difficulties* experienced by me at Harvard in 1987. That affidavit was on the record. When sought to be questioned on the affidavit, Deasy denied having made it.

Appellant

"Mr. Deasy, did you make an Affidavit in the course of these proceedings?"

C. Deasy

"No, My Lord."

Justice Barron

"You did, did you?"

C. Deasy

"I don't recall making an Affidavit, no."

Cyril Deasy was subsequently handed a copy of his affidavit that gave the lie to his denials.

Thirdly, when Michael Mortell, U.C.C. president, was asked the specific question of why a further pension application was solicited in 1989, he could not answer it.

Appellant

"Can you recall what the purpose of another application at that stage was?"

M. Mortell
"No."

Fourthly, Mortell could not recall the request of the 1989 finance committee that led to Dr. Murphy's defamatory report. At the same juncture, he had difficulty in recalling when he became president of U.C.C.

Appellant
"In 1989, I was asked to submit to a further medical examination. Were you aware of that?"
M. Mortell
"I can't say now that I was."
Appellant
"Do you recall as President of University College Cork and a member of the Finance Committee?"
Justice Barron
"When did you become professor?" (The Transcript should read 'President').
M. Mortell
"I think 1989."

Finally, in his summing up, U.C.C. counsel admitted that the independent medical reports from The Malden Hospital of May 10 and 11, 1987, had not been before U.C.C. finance committee, acting as its pension committee.

"It's true that they didn't form part of the documents which were put before the Committee ...."

7 Tantamount to a Farce

The manipulations by university interests in the period 1987 to 1991 had set the scene for an unbalanced presentation in the High Court. In these four years, events within U.C.C. during 1985 and 1986 had been eclipsed, the Harvard dimension had been made to recede, I had been subjected to an illegal and unconstitutional *sheep-dipping* exercise, affidavit evidence had been virtually side-stepped and key witnesses were absenting themselves. The evidence was potentially lost or polluted.

One writer, who had been faced with a similar dilemma, described it in terms of the following analogy:

> "You may remember Ernest Hemingway's novel the Old Man and the Sea. Santiago, the old fisherman, managed to catch a great big fish, a monster fish, so huge that he had to tie it along the boat to bring it back in. By the time Santiago reached shore, the fish long since had been picked apart by sharks. Nothing remained but its skeleton.
>
> Looking back, I can see that this is pretty much the way it turned out when we finally got Clay Shaw to trial in Criminal District Court."

The extract is from J. Garrison, *On the Trail of the Assassins.*

University administrators, who knew most of the facts, withheld or denied them in their testimony. The policy of non-cooperation became blatant as the hearing progressed. At one point, after obvious stonewalling by two university witnesses in succession, presiding Justice Barron remarked that, whereas the operation of the pension committee was central to the case:

> "As far as I am concerned, we have been going through what is tantamount, to a large extent, to a farce."

By affidavit with exhibits dated October 3, 1991, Edmund Cogan, solicitor, had averred that:

> "I say that the issue never arose that the Applicant's pension rights were in any way being compromised by the 1986 High Court Case or by the subsequent settlement made on July 9, 1986."

It was later submitted in the appeal to the Supreme Court that the presiding Judge had erred in law in excluding Mr. Cogan's evidence either by way of affidavit or testimony, and that, this had contributed to the incorrect decision of the High Court.

Whereas the evidence of Edmund Cogan was vital on

the entitlement issue under Statute 79, the evidence of another solicitor, Edmund Hogan, had been vital on the issues of natural and constitutional justice relating to how my pension applications were dealt with.

Edmond Hogan, solicitor, acted in the pension case for me during a period in 1990. He had conducted discovery and examined in detail, over a prolonged period, the documentation thereby obtained. On foot thereof, he swore an affidavit with exhibits dated April 9, 1991. These were also placed on record. In that affidavit, Mr. Hogan had averred that he – as well as Joseph Cuddigan, solicitor, who had been on record before him – believed that natural and constitutional justice had been denied me by U.C.C. finance committee, acting as its pension committee, between 1987 and 1989.

Ultimately, however, the High Court judgment appealed against ignored that evidence. In fact, in the single paragraph that referred to natural and constitutional justice, it reached a totally erroneous conclusion that had been refuted by Mr. Hogan's affidavit evidence.

"The matter was properly considered by the Committee and they had before them, when they made their final decision, a comprehensive report from the Secretary setting out medical reports and other documentation. It is true that the Applicant did not have an opportunity to counter the arguments which were accepted by the Committee nor did he see the report of Dr. Murphy."

Certain themes are evident from the manner in which the vital evidence of the two solicitors, Cogan and Hogan, was dealt with. These include equivocation regarding the evidence relied on, the wrongful exclusion of evidence at the hearing, and the unbalanced, unwarranted and unreasonable manner in which evidence adduced at the hearing was or was not carried forward into the High Court judgment appealed against. Indeed, one of the major grounds of appeal to the Supreme Court was that the High Court hearing had not been either a fair or proper one.

8 Defective High Court Hearing

The issues before the court had been expressly pleaded in the Application for Judicial Review and in the statement of opposition. There were three categories of issue:- first and foremost, the entitlement issue under Statute 79; secondly, adherence or lack of it to natural and constitutional justice leading up to the second refusal of the pension on November 20, 1989; and thirdly, the issue of whether University College Cork was estopped from denying my entitlement by reason of its decisions and conduct in 1985 and 1986.

Having acknowledged jurisdiction, Justice Barron immediately limited the issues to the procedural one.

"I have already told Mr. Linehan, it is no function of mine to see whether he made the right decision, the question is whether the procedures adopted leading to the decision were correct."

This limitation of the issues being heard was repeatedly asserted throughout the hearing. It is anomalous that, having limited the hearing in large part to the procedural issues, Barron's judgment disposed of that issue in only one paragraph.

This criticism is related to the previous one. It bore on a pattern obvious throughout the High Court transcript of rulings of inadmissibility of factual evidence. These rulings of inadmissibility excluded answers to questions relating to, for instance, the following issues:-

- coercion and intimidation of me within U.C.C. in the 1985-1986 period;
- liaison between U.C.C. and Harvard;
- the fabrication of medical evidence in 1989; and
- serious illegality on the part of the reduced U.C.C. finance committee in 1989;

This sweeping exclusion of factual evidence was indeed confirmed by Justice Barron in the following exchange:

Appellant

> *"But as you may appreciate, the background, the factual background is lengthy and complicated."*
> Mr. Justice Barron
> *"I have already ruled that it's inadmissible for the most part."*

A further criticism made on appeal was obviously related to the previous two, and revolved around the conduct of the hearing so as to prevent me from making out my case. It differed from the previous complaint insofar as it bore on the exclusion of entire lines of questioning by refusing to hear witnesses or by shortening their testimony. The pattern now referred to is illustrated by reference to eight witnesses. Thus, the presiding judge restricted the testimony of Edmund Cogan, stood down Michael Vallelly and Pat Fitzpatrick, and indicated that there was no point in calling Alphonsus O'Brien. The evidence of these witnesses bore on the raison d'etre of the case. Barron ruled:

> *"I have ruled, I am not going to allow you to reopen this matter through witnesses, so far as the affidavits are concerned – I haven't read any – because this trial is before me on oral evidence. Now you may stand down." (to P. Fitzpatrick).*

The foregoing four witnesses would not have been adverse to me. When attempts were made to adduce the same evidence from university administrators, these also led to interruptions or the curtailment of their testimony.

In the High Court it transpired that, in law, U.C.C.'s statement of opposition was reduced to a trivial, indeed, nonsensical point. As expressed by Sean O'Leary, U.C.C. counsel:-

> *"Now, that is not my statement of opposition – my statement of opposition is basically that Mr. Linehan resigned and he did not retire."*

On appeal, I contended that this defence consisted of a distinction without a difference, a play on words that moreover had validity neither in semantics nor in fact. The refusal to hear witnesses on the circumstances preceding and surrounding the settlement of July 9, 1986, precluded me from meeting the net point in U.C.C.'s statement of opposition. Michael Mortell was asked:-

"Did the negotiations involve various pressures?"

Justice Barron ruled:-

"That is a question you cannot ask."

I was contending that, at the behest of a reduced finance committee, I had been subjected to an illegal premeditated sheep-dipping exercise in 1989 that violated my fundamental rights.

The testimony of Aidan Moran, U.C.C. registrar, was interrupted in relation to these issues. I sought also to open the issues of fraud and illegality in the 1989 period with Michael Enright, U.C.C. solicitor. A central point was that U.C.C. had received, at least as late as 1988, copies of medical reports from The Malden Hospital, Massachusetts, that indicated serious personal injuries. In open correspondence between the solicitors on both sides in 1989, that receipt had been denied and a spurious solicitation was then made for another pension application. This also was refused in November 20, 1989. However, the reduced U.C.C. finance committee had used the renewed application as a plausible basis to compile a defamatory report from Dr. M. Murphy.

By curtailing investigation of the activities of the U.C.C. finance committee in that way, and disposing of the issues of fact and law that arose in one paragraph of the judgment, it was submitted that both the High Court hearing and judgment had by-passed a great deal of serious illegality directed against me.

Further, by adopting the tenor of Dr. Murphy's report in the judgment, a grave miscarriage has been done to me. What it amounted to was that, if a person can be tricked into meeting a psychiatrist, and the latter, without any basis, draws a report that hints at possible or future psychosis, that person can be destroyed by being branded a psychotic in the High Court. That is one of the things that had happened in the case in the High Court.

In the same vein, the High Court transcript also proved the curtailment of lines of questioning that would have established the true causes and nature of my ill health. Dr. O'Connell's testimony was interrupted on that basis.

Justice Barron

"Mr. Linehan, it seems to me that there are two things that you have to establish in relation to health, if it is material, which, as I have already indicated, I don't think it is. One is you became ill during your period of employment, and the other matter is that the ill-health was going to be permanent. So, the fact that the ill-health may have been caused by heavy workload is totally immaterial, please don't ask those sort of questions to anyone."

The pattern of disallowing certain lines of questioning by refusing to hear witnesses, or by disallowing their testimony, was in fact constantly shown throughout the High Court transcript.

Apart from those exclusions, it was submitted that the transcript of testimony proved a number of other more general patterns relating to the attitude adopted by the presiding judge to me and witnesses likely to be favourable to me on the one hand, and to U.C.C. administrator witnesses and the interests of that institution, as well as Harvard, on the other hand.

In broad terms, it was submitted that a number of general rulings, directions and other various interventions by Justice Barron during the hearing could reasonably be taken as indicating a greater concern for maintaining the interests of U.C.C. and Harvard than in vindicating my legal rights. It was contended that several passages identified in the transcript indicated a distinct antipathy by Justice Barron to the case being made by me.

One of the identified instances may be taken to illustrate. After I had supplied a date to a witness, at the suggestion of the presiding judge, the latter then intervened as follows:-

*"That is all in the documents, why are you wasting time?
Half the time in this court is wasted by you because you are
asking questions which are totally unnecessary."*

It was contended that there was a very serious wrong-doing in the background to this case on the part of certain university administrators. It can be summarised that the presiding judge was not disposed to having that wrong-doing brought to light. For instance, having adverted to coercion and intimidation in the 1985 to 1986 period that had forced my retirement within the meaning of Statute 79, I was quickly interrupted:-

*"The evidence may well show the serious allegations you are
making are correct, but at the moment there is nothing to
suggest that. I would just like to point out to you that you
are harming your case with these unnecessary allegations."*

The failure by U.C.C. administrators to comply with subpoena created obvious difficulty in their examination. The presiding judge refused on one occasion to allow me to make up for this non-compliance by supplying one such witness with copy documents. I, rather than, as one would have expected, the non-complying witness, incurred judicial censure:-

Mr. Justice Barron

"Well then if that is so, your behaviour is inexcusable."

Appellant

"Well I am being put in a situation where because witnesses are not complying with the subpoena -"

Mr. Justice Barron

*"Look, please stop arguing with the court and get on with
relevant questions."*

The pattern of inhibitive interventions by Barron restricted the scope of the hearing even more so than his narrow definition of the issues at hearing and the sweeping exclusion of factual evidence might suggest. For instance, the failure of U.C.C. administrators to bring documentation to court on foot of subpoena was virtually endorsed rather than censured.

Justice Barron

"No, but if you have had discovery you know what documents exist and you could have asked for them to be brought, you can't just ask the witness to put a whole lot of books, or bring them up to Dublin."

Appellant

"Well, Your Honour, I have had to do that for four years."

On occasions, the interventions by the presiding judge in relation to U.C.C. administrator witnesses effectively amounted to answering questions on their behalf. I had not been formally requested for medical evidence in the context of the 1987 pension claims and applications – I maintained that U.C.C. finance committee did not do so in order to avoid being put on formal notice of the personal injuries received at Harvard as indicated by the independent medical reports from The Malden Hospital, Massachusetts, of May 1987. When this line of questioning was opened with Cyril Deasy, deputy finance officer, U.C.C., Justice Barron intervened on his behalf:-

Justice Barron

"As far as you are aware, whatever you required was asked for?"

Deasy

"That's correct, My Lord."

Justice Barron

"And obtained."

Deasy

"Absolutely, My Lord, yes."

My questions were then cut short.

Justice Barron

"He has already told you everything he knows."

Again when the crucial issue of liaison between U.C.C. and Harvard was sought to be raised with Michael Enright, U.C.C. solicitor, it was the presiding judge rather than U.C.C. counsel who first made an objection of privilege on his behalf:-

Justice Barron

"Well that would be privileged if they had done."
Mr. O'Leary
"My Lord, I don't know what this witness ...."
Justice Barron
"No, if they had made inquiries for the purposes of this case it would be privileged."
Mr. O'Leary
"It would, My Lord, it would."

Key U.C.C. administrator witnesses were readily excused from attending court on the basis of medical certificates that had been previously challenged for reasons stated in writing by me.

On the sixth day of the hearing, Justice Barron effectively aborted the hearing. The attendance of numerous key witnesses was dispensed with en masse. Some of these such as Doctors Carmody and Khudados were medical witnesses independent of U.C.C. and Harvard who could have testified to the true causes and nature of my ill health, and who would have refuted categorically the smear arising from Doctor Murphy's defamatory report of October 3, 1989.

Bryan McMahon, solicitor, was a principal witness. Dispensing with his attendance was a clear mark of the bogus nature of the proceedings at this point.

In thus aborting the hearing after six days of hearing witnesses, Barron expressed that his overriding concern was for the interests of U.C.C.

"You have some idea that you can prolong this case for as long as it seems to suit you. I am here to do justice and that means not only do I consider your case, I also have to consider the college's case and it's hardly just to the college to allow matters to continue, apparently without cease. It's a matter of great expense to the college that matters are going on."

In sum, it was contended in the appeal to the Supreme Court that the contrasting patterns of judicial interventions during the hearing relating to me on the one hand, and U.C.C. on the other hand, proved that the hearing was not conducted in an objective and impartial manner.

9 President's Testimony

One redeeming feature of the High Court hearing was that testimony proving my pension case was adduced in the course of it from two senior administrators of U.C.C. throughout the relevant period. Michael Mortell was U.C.C. registrar between about 1980 and 1989, when he became president. He was asked whether I had qualified for a pension under Statute 79 in 1985 and 1986:-

Appellant

"In your opinion, Professor Mortell, did you think that I would have qualified, did qualify for retirement on ill-health at that time?"

M. Mortell

"Yes, that was talking about strictly – that was one of the three options as I heard the judge say, that was put to you before any settlement has taken place."

Appellant

"Perhaps I will ask you then, had you seen the medical reports at that stage?"

M. Mortell

"Yes."

Justice Barron

"You had?"

M. Mortell

"Yes."

It was submitted that the above testimony was one of several pieces of evidence on record that proved the entitlement and estoppel issues in the case in my favour.

It was a basic thesis of mine that the pension claimed had not been paid, not for factual or legal reasons, but in the context of the cover-up commenced by certain U.C.C. and Harvard administrators in May, 1987.

Michael Kelleher had been U.C.C. finance officer and secretary throughout the relevant period, and had had a pivotal role in events during the 1985-1991 period. Certain of his testimony clearly proved the inadequacy of the evidence that was formally before the finance committee, acting as the pension committee, that repeated on November 20, 1989, the 1987 refusal of a Statute 79 pension to me:-

S. O'Leary

"But I take it from Friday the 20th of November, 1989 you were both secretary and ...."

M. Kelleher

"Yes, that is correct."

S. O'Leary

"I see. Now do you remember, do you remember what was before the committee on that occasion in terms of documentation?"

M. Kelleher

"There was an extensive file of correspondence led by a memorandum which I wrote myself, dated the 17th November and attached to that was all the relevant material going back to 1987, for the convenience of, most of this, if not all of this, they would have before ...."

Justice Barron

"Perhaps you would consider Mr. Kelleher that since it was the larger pension – was in relation to a period during employment, that you didn't in the memorandum circulate it to the members about his position during the period, that period, do you see the point."

M. Kelleher

"I do, My Lord, yes."

Justice Barron

"I mean if he was looking for a pension in relation to facts that occurred before the 31st of June 1987 it seems that members of the Committee could have been given information about that period ...."

The testimony of Michael Mortell and Michael Kelleher was highlighted on the crucial issues in the pension case. Although these were two of the core members of the finance committee that has withheld the pension claimed, it is illuminating that even their testimony proved my pension case in its entirety.

10 High Court Decision

The High Court judgment of January 31, 1992, ran to twenty one pages in length. In referring to the 1986 case, the judgment noted that:-

"In the Spring of 1985 the Applicant applied for a sabbatical year in order to study at Harvard University. He had previously made a number of applications for such leave all of which had been refused. This application was likewise refused.... In July 1985 at a meeting with the College President and Secretary he was given a number of options whereby his employment might be terminated....

From that time onwards, the College authorities regarded him as being unfit for his duties. After some steps which were contested by the Applicant, he was suspended in February 1986. This led to further unsuccessful negotiation and ultimately on the 27th March 1986 proceedings were commenced by the Applicant against the College ...."

This account of events within U.C.C. in 1985 and 1986 did not expressly refer to the personal vendetta that had given rise to the unlawful activities that were referred to. Again one would need to be both a discerning and knowledgeable reader to infer the duress and intimidation that is referred to in the phrase:-

"After some steps which were contested by the Applicant ...."

It had been repeatedly proved that these steps had consisted of a premeditated and sustained attack on my tenure, reputation, and other property rights. Later, it was admitted by letter dated September 16, 1987, by Michael Enright, U.C.C. solicitor, that the aforesaid steps and the resulting retirement:-

".... was due to the fact that (I) wanted to go to Harvard."

The High Court judgment of January 31, 1992, proceeded on page 7 to recite the Order of the High Court made on July 10, 1986, by Justice Murphy on foot of the settlement. This order read as follows:-

By Consent IT IS ORDERED AND ADJUDGED that the Plaintiff do recover against the Defendant the sum of £40,000.00 for damages together with a sum of £5,000.00 by way of contribution towards the Plaintiff's costs.

The judgment continued on page 7 as follows:-

"By letter dated the 18th of July 1986 the Applicant irrevocably tendered his resignation from his position as College lecturer at University College Cork with effect from 30th of June 1987 in accordance with the terms of settlement ...."

The judgment on page 7 recited two other proceedings that followed from the 1986 High Court case and in which I also succeeded against U.C.C. Its administrators had sought in the taxation context to detract from the High Court settlement and order of July, 1986. However, the Revenue Adjudication Office had held on December 22, 1986, that the £40,000.00 damages were not liable to income tax.

Subsequently, a further adjudication of the unlawful activities against me by U.C.C. law department and administration in 1985 and 1986 was made by Cork Circuit Court on January 15, 1990. This ruled against the revenue commissioners that my U.C.C. salary, paid while at Harvard, constituted part of the damages obtained in the 1986 High Court case. Accordingly, it had not been liable to income tax.

The High Court judgment of 1992 referred only in a fleeting way to the critical period at Harvard between August, 1986, and June, 1987. At page 7, it is noted that:-

"Following upon the settlement the Applicant took up the place which had been offered to him by Harvard University. He completed his course there and was awarded an LL.M. Degree. Unfortunately in the course of that year he .... was admitted to hospital with suspected heart trouble ...."

The judgment did not mention the reasons for the

admission. The academic dons were treated as if they were above and beyond the law. That was so, notwithstanding the volume of evidence before the court.

In thus failing to grasp the nettle, the judgment ultimately avoided the most obvious proposition, namely, if one's employer directly, or indirectly through others, causes incapacity during the period of employment, that is a most obvious basis for providing a pension based on incapacity.

The High Court judgment, on pages 8 and 9, proceeded to transcribe letters dated July 26 and 28, 1987, from myself and Joseph Cuddigan, solicitor, to U.C.C. finance office. It then proceeded to synopsise the two types of incapacity pensions provided for in the U.C.C. statutes. The larger, that is a matter of entitlement, is payable for incapacity arising during U.C.C. employment. The smaller, that is discretionary, may be payable if incapacity arises after the cessation of U.C.C. employment.

No doubt existed as to the pension that was claimed in July, 1987. As a result of the retaliatory abuse at Harvard that followed the 1986 High Court case against U.C.C., I had been hospitalised twice in the last thirteen weeks of thirteen years of U.C.C. employment with suspected heart attacks and other injuries.

Having referred to the two types of incapacity pension provided for in the U.C.C. statutes, the High Court judgment continued by referring to the reply made to the claim for a pension made in July, 1987:-

"The College authorities replied on the 17th September 1987 by letter to the effect that

'The Pension Committee has decided to recommend that the provisions regarding the preservation of pensions be applied to Mr. Linehan.'

This was a reference to a pension under Statute 108. The letter also made it clear that entitlement did not arise until age 60."

The letter dated September 17, 1987, issued from the finance office of U.C.C. of which Michael Kelleher was finance officer and secretary. Remarkably, it made no reference to either of the two types of disability pension, but instead referred to the pension payable at the normal retirement age of 60. This letter signified that Harvard and U.C.C. administrators had then resolved on a cover-up. The letter had been written on foot of a meeting of U.C.C. finance committee, that had acted as a pension committee, on September 14, 1987.

The High Court judgment referred to a letter dated September 29, 1987, by Joseph Cuddigan, solicitor, to U.C.C. finance office that threatened District Court proceedings within 14 days unless the pension claimed was paid retroactive to July, 1987, i.e. the month after both my return from Harvard and the cessation of my U.C.C. employment. The judgment continued as follows:-

"Nothing came of this further letter and proceedings were commenced in the District Court to recover a pension. These proceedings were brought by way of civil process claiming a sum of £110.00 for the period 4th October, 1987, to 10th October, 1987, in respect of arrears of disability pension due by the Defendant to the Plaintiff. These proceedings never came to hearing."

Here again, the High Court judgment circumvented highly pertinent facts, namely, *why* no hearing took place in Cork District Court between 1987 and 1989. The failure to secure a hearing resulted from the refusal by key university witnesses to come to court, and the refusal in other respects to cooperate in the matter of evidence, such as by refusals to comply with notices to admit facts and documents.

The High Court judgment of January 31, 1992, had by-passed all this evidence, and more to similar effect, in the single sentence previously quoted:-

"[The Cork District Court] *proceedings never came to hearing.*"

Again, the High Court judgment made no reference to any of the blatant misrepresentations used by U.C.C. finance committee through their solicitors in order to procure the 1989 pension application. For instance, with letter dated July 15, 1988, Joseph Cuddigan, solicitor had forwarded a notice to admit documents to the U.C.C. solicitors and enclosed the medical reports from The Malden Hospital, Massachusetts, of May, 1987, that had arisen by reason of the abuse at Harvard in the previous months. Ten months later, Michael Enright, solicitor, on behalf of U.C.C. denied receipt of that medical evidence in a letter to Joseph Cuddigan dated May 19, 1989, as follows:-

".... Mr. Linehan has apparently suggested that medical evidence has been submitted to us but this is not correct."

In the course of the High Court hearing, Sean O'Leary, U.C.C. counsel, had acknowledged the aforesaid critical misrepresentation by Michael Enright:-

".... after the 1987 decision proceedings in the District Court .... certain documents including medical documents, documents with a medical source were sent by the solicitor, for the university, in the course of that preparation .... we are accepting that."

The High Court judgment made no reference whatever to the fraud that had attended the U.C.C. solicitation in 1989 of a second pension application.

Certain elements of the fraud that attended the solicitation on behalf of university interests in 1989 of a second obviously unnecessary pension application have already been adverted to. A further element pertained to the speciality of Dr. Murphy and to his independence from both U.C.C. and Harvard. I had assumed that Dr. Murphy was a physician competent to diagnose the injuries sustained at Harvard in 1987. I had also been induced to believe that he was independent of the two interested universities - that the medical examination was to be by a doctor practising in Dublin was taken to imply same.

Dr. Murphy's U.C.C. affiliation had become a matter

of record during the High Court hearing in 1991. The following exchange took place during the testimony of Aidan Moran, who was then U.C.C. registrar:-

Appellant

"Is Dr. Murray [transcript should read Murphy] *a graduate of U.C.C.?"*

Justice Barron

"Look, it is not necessary to ask this witness those questions, he doesn't, it is not an issue."

Appellant

"Well am I to take it that I may ask other witnesses that question?"

Justice Barron

"No, you may take it that you may not ask a question when it's not in issue, it is not being contested that Dr. Murray [Transcript should read Murphy] *was a graduate of U.C.C. therefore its unnecessary to go on about it."*

Also during the High Court hearing, after I began to probe the evidence relating to networking in 1989 between Michael Kelleher, U.C.C. finance officer, and university affiliated medical personnel who had intervened irregularly at that time, Sean O'Leary, U.C.C. counsel, himself stated one of the main points that my questioning was designed to bring out:-

S. O'Leary

"With respect, I doubt very much that the 1989 medical condition and the difficulties have anything to do with employment that terminated on the 30th June, 1987."

At pages 14 and 15, the judgment referred to the recourse to the High Court in 1990, as well as the reliefs that were sought in the pleadings.

Having recited the statutory provisions, the judgment at pages 16 and 17 recited what Justice Barron had identified as the real issues in the case:-

"The grounds upon which relief was sought were lengthy and complex. However the real issues in the case reduced themselves to three:

(1)   *was the decision on the 20th November 1989 reached in accordance with fair procedures?;*

(2)   *was the Applicant entitled to a pension pursuant to the provisions of Statute 79?;*

(3)   *did the settlement dated the 1st July 1986 estop the Applicant from seeking this or any other pension?"*

Having intoned from the defamatory report of Dr. Murphy dated October 3, 1989, the judgment proceeded to the decision in the case. In fact and in law, it would have been logical for a substantial portion of the judgment to have been given over to the issue of natural and constitutional justice. Instead, without any reference to any of the numerous authorities on the subject, the judgment summarily disposed of these issues in the following two short paragraphs:

"In considering the issues raised, it seems to me the fairness or otherwise by which the decision of 20th of November 1989 was reached is immaterial. The award of the pension does not depend upon discretion. If the Applicant comes within the terms of the statute, it is admitted that he is entitled to the pension as of right.

The Applicant in any event did not establish lack of fair procedures. The matter was properly considered by the Committee and they had before them when they made their final decision a comprehensive report from the secretary setting out medical reports and other documentation. It is true that the Applicant did not have an opportunity to counter the arguments which were accepted by the Committee nor did he see the report of Dr. Murphy. However, it is clear from the correspondence that he was made aware of the manner in which his application would be dealt with and he acquiesced in that form of procedure. Certainly he made no application to be heard before the Committee or anything of that nature. While there are cases where the tribunal should put an Applicant more fully in the picture as to the matters it is taking into account, this is not one of them."

In order to exculpate U.C.C. administrators from an extended four and a half year period of serious criminal and unlawful cover-up activity, it had been necessary in the High Court judgment to ignore governing law and to circumvent the substantial evidence of wrongdoing that had been adduced.

Having exonerated U.C.C. administrators in a quick and sweeping manner, the High Court judgment finally disposed also, summarily, of the core entitlement issue in the case.

The judgment was read in open court in the High Court in Dublin at 10.30 a.m. on January 31, 1992.

After Justice Barron had cleared the U.C.C. finance committee of prolonged unlawful and serious criminal activity, my anger was prompting me to leave the court as a token response.

The judgment was, however, concluded before I had finally made that decision.

In the written copy of the judgment, the entitlement issue is dealt with on pages 20 and 21:-

"Consideration of the terms of Statute 79 suggests that pension is payable to someone who is obliged to retire by reason of an incapacity which is likely to be permanent. In the present case there was undoubtedly evidence from which the appropriate authority might have so decided. However, neither the Applicant nor the Respondents made that case at the time."

The last sentence was clearly incorrect, and the evidence adduced had proved that.

"Further the pension is payable to a person who is compelled to retire by reason of incapacity. Here the Applicant retired by agreement."

Again the last sentence was clearly wrong. I had retired under unlawful duress and intimidation by a small envious and malicious clique within U.C.C. law department.

There was no mistaking the first punch-line in the judgment:-

"In the circumstances the relief claimed will be disallowed."

Neither was there any mistaking the second punch-line.

This awarded the costs to U.C.C.

If I had previously entertained any lingering doubts about my mistake in pursuing a career in law at the innocent age of seventeen, and my other major mistake at that time in attending university, they were finally dispelled at that moment.

11 Whitewash for the Dons

The finance committee had been taken by surprise by judicial review proceedings for a pension. Its actions in 1989, thus fell for consideration by reference to, at a minimum, natural and constitutional justice.

According to their testimony, the finance committee never sought medical evidence from either Doctors Dineen or O'Connell.

At the request of U.C.C. finance Office, my applications and claims for a pension between July, 1987, and July, 1989, had been processed by Joseph Cuddigan, solicitor. Through much of that period, Isabelle Sutton, B.L., acted as counsel. Their testimony proves that the finance committee was non communicative.

Appellant
"Again in 1987, Mr. Cuddigan, subsequent to the refusal of the pension, were you furnished with evidence of medical evidence on which the refusal was based?"
J. Cuddigan
"No, My Lord."
Appellant
"Did you have the opportunity to be aware of any evidence which the Committee had at that time?"
J. Cuddigan
"No, My Lord."
Appellant
"Can you recall, Mr. Cuddigan, in relation to 1987 whether

any reasons were given for the refusal of the pension?"

J. Cuddigan

"No."

Appellant

"At that time, again, were you informed of any procedure of appealing the refusal?"

J. Cuddigan

"No."

Isabelle Sutton had acted as counsel for much of the period between 1987 and 1989. Since carriage of the pension applications was conducted through my legal representatives for much of that period, some communication with Miss Sutton might have been expected. Her testimony discounted any such communication.

Appellant

"Did the Pension Committee afford you an opportunity for any communication on the matter?"

I. Sutton

"No, I had absolutely no dealings with the Pension Committee for Mr. Cuddigan, Solicitor."

The secretive and furtive workings of the finance committee in 1989 was also confirmed by my testimony under cross-examination by Sean O'Leary.

S. O'Leary

"Did you want to be heard by the Committee?"

Appellant

"Certainly."

S. O'Leary

"What additional information did you wish to convey to the committee prior to the making of their decision?"

Appellant

"Well, for starters I didn't know what information the committee had, so I don't think I am in a position to know what information to provide the committee with. There had been a wall of solicitors for two years." "

In answer to Justice Barron's invitation to comment on events in 1989, I testified as to my consistent views of the manipulations by the finance committee in that year.

Justice Barron

"This is a submission. Is there anything about the interpretation he has been seeking to put on the letters, you feel you didn't explain yourself properly, you want to re-explain anything like that?"

Appellant

"....the Pension Committee had in its possession everything available except a death cert since May 1987. I believe that the other side then represented and attempted to fabricate medical evidence arising from 1987 that showed that in the last months of my employment I suffered personal injuries at Harvard and I believe that the entire exercise was an attempt to cover up the background."

Michael Mortell was U.C.C. registrar until he became president in February, 1989, succeeding the late Tadgh O'Ciardha. His testimony corroborated certain of the irregularities that were proved by the documentation. Mortell was queried relating to the 1989 application.

Appellant

"Do you recall what the purpose of another application at that stage was?"

M. Mortell

"No."

Appellant

"In 1989, professor, I was asked to submit to a further medical examination. Were you aware of that?"

M. Mortell

"I can't say now that I was"

Appellant

"Do you recall at that time being advised or considering whether I or my representatives should be informed as to the difficulties or the issues that my application and claim raised?"

M. Mortell

"I just don't understand that question. I don't know what it means."

Efforts to question Michael Mortell about the Harvard

dimension were cut short.

Appellant

"When did you become aware, professor, that I had difficulties at Harvard University?"

Justice Barron

"That doesn't arise, it is certainly not an appropriate question – presumes some knowledge.

The set-up of me with Dr. Murphy at the behest of the reduced 1989 U.C.C. finance committee was emphasised during Aidan Moran's testimony. I made the following submission in the course of same:-

Appellant

"....and then in 1989, when the proceedings were withdrawn in the District Court and when U.C.C. was put on notice that the case was transferred to the High Court, that the relevant administrators by a process involving fraud and misrepresentation practised on me and my legal representatives during the period between March and October of 1989, set out, deliberately, to fabricate medical evidence of a psychological nature."

Justice Barron

"Very well, we'll leave it at that, I got it slightly wrong ...."

Throughout the hearing, Justice Barron had consistently emphasised the workings of the finance committee. That was in no way reflected in his judgment appealed against.

12 A Wad of Notes

Psychopolitics is a highly developed science, as is indicated by the following quotations from an address given by Beria to American Students at the Lenin university school in Moscow and that is included in K. Goff, Manual of Instructions of Psychopolitical Warfare:-

"American students at the Lenin University, I welcome your attendance at these classes on Psychopolitics.

Psychopolitics is an important if less known division of Geopolitics. It is less known because it must necessarily deal with highly educated personnel, the very top strata of "mental healing" .... You must labour until every doctor and psychiatrist is either a psychopolitician or an unwilling assistant to our aims .... With the institutions for the insane you have in your country prisons which can hold a million persons and can hold them without civil rights or any hope of freedom. And upon these people can be practiced shock and surgery so that never again will they draw a sane breath ...."

You must dominate as respected men the fields of psychiatry and psychology. You must dominate the hospitals and universities ..."

Psychopolitics had been referred to tacitly during the High Court hearing. The allusions were brief.

Joseph Cuddigan, solicitor, and Michael Keating, Harvard Mediator, had communicated between July, 1987, and January, 1988, on the issue of compensation for the personal injuries arising from the savage retaliatory abuse at Harvard in the preceding months. By letter dated September 10, 1987, Cuddigan had written to Keating as follows:-

"I understand that, when you last spoke to Mr. Linehan on June 4th, 1987, you requested that a figure be mentioned in correspondence on the basis of how this case might be settled. Mr. Linehan's future prospects have been severely affected by the Harvard experience and his hearing would appear to have been diminished. Hence a sum of £200,000 should be sought by way of compensation."

In Keating's reply to that letter, the issue of psychopolitics was first raised in the context of it being used as a defence. He quoted a saying in his letter dated September 25, 1987:

"Just because I'm paranoid doesn't mean that someone isn't out to get me."

In sum, the issue of psychopolitics had first been mooted by a Harvard fixer in Autumn, 1987, after the question of compensation had started to be defined.

A major theme of the appeal was that, from the start of the case in 1987 to the present, the defence had been largely motivated and fuelled by American dollars.

It was proved clearly in the appeal presentation that a false inducement, fraud and misrepresentation were resorted to in 1989 to discredit me by means of what it was contended was a commissioned report from Dr. Murphy dated October 3, 1989.

In his closing submissions, Sean O'Leary admitted that the medical reports from The Malden Hospital, Massachusetts, dated May 10, 1987, that marked the consequences of the abuse at Harvard, were not formally before the finance committee, acting as the pension committee. That admission was striking, given that those reports constituted independent medical evidence of serious personal injuries. In keeping with the policy of both Harvard and U.C.C. since 1987, O'Leary referred dismissively to the reports:-

".... I think Mr. Linehan had another point that he put to Mr. Enright, that during the course of 1987 proceedings, the court, the District Court Proceedings, that it gave certain documents to University College Cork which I think basically consisted of a wad of notes, notes from a hospital in the United States, and that these documents should have been considered in the examination of the 19- in 1987, of his position with regard to that .... it's true that they didn't form part of the documents which were put before the committee ...."

In concluding, it can be summarised that the gravamen of the appeal were twofold. First, the High Court failed to deal with the pension case adequately. Secondly, it failed to glean and address the calculated premeditated psychopolitical wrongs done to me in the period from 1987 onwards.

These wrongs can be gauged by the following letter from Reinier Kraakman, professor at Harvard law school, dated May 22, 1987.

"
HARVARD LAW SCHOOL
Cambridge, Massachusetts 01138

Mr. Denis Linehan,   *May 22, 1987*
220 Holmes Hall,
18 Everett Street,
Cambridge, MA 02138
Dear Mr. Linehan,
I have received your seminar paper and am pleased to inform you that you have successfully completed all requirements for "Theories of Firms and Markets." In addition, I find that the quality of your seminar contribution easily satisfies the standard of the Harvard LLM program.

> *Sincerely,*
> *Reinier Kraakman*
> *Visiting Professor of Law"*

My official grades from Harvard, dated June 11, 1987, verified, even more comprehensively than some of the other evidence, that I was thinking very clearly and to the mark at Harvard in 1987.

HARVARD LAW SCHOOL
Cambridge, Massachusetts 01138

Record of *Linehan, Denis Martin*
Degree received LL.M. 1987 June 11

Entrance Status: Graduate - LL.M.

Law School Credits	Date	Mark	Credit
Comparative Legal Education	12/86	A-	2
International Law: Int. Commercial Arbitration	12/86	B+	2
International Law: Transnational Legal Prob.	12/86	B+	2
Comparative Law: Civil Law Systems	1/87	B+	2
Alternative Methods in Dispute Resolution	5/87	Cr.	2

Sem: Theories of Firms & Markets	5/87	B+	2
Written Work Von Mehren	5/87	B+	2
Total Credits			16

13 Cover–Up Sequence

In the appeal submission to the Irish Supreme Court, it was maintained that Harvard and U.C.C. administrators had undertaken a cover-up following my confinement in intensive care at The Malden Hospital, Massachusetts, in May, 1987.

Following are the basic contentions that were maintained in my characterisation of U.C.C. finance committee as a poisonous clam in the period 1987 to 1992. My fundamental contention was that at least two U.C.C. insider administrators were complicit in or knowledgeable of the retaliatory abuse at Harvard in 1987. Part of the proofs offered consisted of the High Court testimony of Michael Mortell.

Mortell was U.C.C. registrar prior to 1989, when he became president. His testimony confirmed that U.C.C. finance committee had been anticipating litigation from 1987 onwards.

Shortly after the independent medical reports from The Malden Hospital, Massachusetts of May, 1987, marked the onset of my personal injuries, the corresponding insider administrators at Harvard notified their U.C.C. counterparts.

Correspondence clearly marked the Harvard response to the confinement in Malden Hospital. By letter dated May 5, 1987, David O'Connor of Massachusetts Mediation Service had written to me as follows:

"In accordance with our telephone conversation, I have

enclosed a copy of our brochure and our annual report.

I look forward to talking with you on Tuesday, May 26 at 10a.m. here at my office."

That meeting never took place. On May 10, 1987, I was confined in intensive care at The Malden Hospital. As soon as possible thereafter, by letter dated May 19, 1987, that is also on record, Frederick Snyder, administrator of Harvard's graduate program, intimated by letter that I should return to Ireland forthwith:-

" .... I hope you have a pleasant journey to Ireland in the next several days, and wish you all the best there."

My pension claim and applications were refused peremptorily by a finance committee, acting as a pension committee, controlled by the insider administrators concerned in September 1987. That was clearly proved by the minutes of U.C.C. finance committee dated September 14, 1987.

" .... The Committee noted that Mr. Linehan, after protracted negotiations and in consideration of a considerable compensation package, had voluntarily resigned. Accordingly, his pension entitlement would be a deferred pension...."

Harvard instructed Michael Keating, who had been in communication with Joseph Cuddigan, solicitor, to break off communications as soon as the pension case had progressed in Cork District Court.

Keating had thus formally exited, leaving only the germ of an idea, i.e., a psychopolitical defence to all litigation.

Proceedings in Cork District Court in 1987 and 1988 were circumvented by avoidance by insider U.C.C. administrators of witness summonses and by a policy otherwise of non-cooperation. For instance, by letter dated November 8th, 1988, from Cyril Deasy to Michael Enright, solicitor, it was stated that:-

".... Professor Mortell has not been involved in any way with this claim and does not see that he has anything whatsoever to contribute as a witness."

In order to maintain secrecy to the greatest extent possible in anticipation of personal injuries litigation, the composition of U.C.C. finance committee was reduced in numbers to such an extent that the extraordinary step was taken of co-opting Michael Kelleher, secretary, as a member of the committee in order to make up a quorum of five.

Mr. O'Leary
"Had you become a member of the Committee at that stage as distinct from the Secretary?"
Mr. Kelleher
"Since February 1989 I was, I was a full member of the Committee, yes."
Mr. O'Leary
"Prior to that you had acted ...."
Mr. Kelleher
"As secretary."
Mr. O'Leary
"As secretary only."

When Joseph Cuddigan, solicitor, notified U.C.C. solicitors in March, 1989, of High Court proceedings, without specifying what the proceedings would relate to, U.C.C. insider administrators anticipated a major personal injuries case.

The correspondence from this period is illustrative. It shows Michael Enright, U.C.C. solicitor, to profess that he does not know what proceedings are in question. Enright wrote to Michael Kelleher, U.C.C. secretary, in the following terms:-

"I enclose for your attention a copy letter from Joseph S. Cuddigan & Company. I haven't any idea what proceedings they are talking about, but have declined to accept service and said that the proceedings should be served directly on you."

Correspondence that was on record, as well as testimony from the High Court, proved that a number of obvious lies were propagated by the U.C.C. finance committee between March and October, 1989 to the intent of concocting defamatory evidence. Thus, the false inducement for the obviously unnecessary pension application in 1989 came through the medium of Michael Enright. By letter dated April 10, 1989, Joseph Cuddigan, solicitor, wrote to Miss Isabelle Sutton, B.L., in the following terms:-

> *".... Mr. Enright suggested that we should make a formal application to the pension committee and without going so far as to say so certainly the impression was conveyed we would be pushing an open door. I discussed this matter with Denis and he brought to my attention that he had already made such an application."*

In order to provide a plausible basis for fabricating such evidence, it was decided to solicit a further pension application, in the course of which I could be requested to submit to a medical examination. To that end, Enright's letter to Cuddigan, dated May 19, 1989, contained two false assertions:-

(a) *".... Mr. Linehan has not made any application to U.C.C. for a pension,"* and

(b) *"Mr. Linehan has apparently suggested that medical evidence has been submitted to us but this is not correct."*

Having ignored the pension claim for nearly two years, U.C.C. finance committee actively sought another application in 1989. Having received same on July 14, 1989, it was used as a guise to justify a medical examination that resulted in a scurrilous defamatory report. Statute 79 contemplated only medical evidence for the period of employment. In my circumstances, that was October, 1974 - June 1987. Medical evidence in 1989 was clearly irrelevant to the pension that had been sought since July, 1987. During the High Court hearing, Sean O'Leary, U.C.C. counsel, inadvertently conceded this.

Mr. O'Leary

> *"With respect, I doubt very much that the 1989 medical condition and the difficulties have anything to do with employment that terminated on the 30th of June, 1987."*

I was duped into meeting Dr. Murphy who wrote a commissioned report dated October 3, 1989.

Until I met him in Dublin, I did not discover that Dr. Murphy was a U.C.C. graduate. One of the university misrepresentations used in fabricating false medical evidence in 1989, namely, that the examination would be carried out by an independent doctor, was belied at the High Court hearing.

My weight had reached 19.5 stone by August, 1989, and I had signed myself into a general hospital for physiotherapy and dietary treatments. Michael Kelleher, U.C.C. finance officer and secretary, saw an opportunity in that episode, and arranged that Dr. LeGear call on me in the hospital.

No legal explanation is possible of how Dr. LeGear's home details came to be on the letter from Michael Kelleher to me dated September 25, 1989. An unsuccessful effort was made by U.C.C. counsel to imply that those details were given by Joseph Cuddigan, solicitor.

Mr. O'Leary

"I must put it to you in passing, the evidence will be, if necessary, that that information came to the attention of College authorities through Mr. Enright and Mr. Enright got the information from you."

Mr. Cuddigan

"I can't comment on that, My Lord."

Strand by strand, the attempted cover-up was being unravelled.

Having secured Dr. Murphy's report, that had been the objective of the solicitation of the unnecessary 1989 pension application, U.C.C. finance committee again peremptorily refused this application on November 20, 1989.

U.C.C. and Harvard insider administrators, being in anticipation of a major personal injuries action, were surprised by the judicial review proceedings for a pension that were commenced in February, 1990. A bland statement of opposition was filed in reply by Sean O'Leary, a former member of U.C.C. governing body. When pressed at the High Court hearing, it transpired that the opposition to the pension that had been made since 1987 was put as turning upon an absurd distinction without a difference.

Mr. Justice Barron

" .... Mr. O'Leary, what is the basis of your opposition to this case?"

Mr. O'Leary

"... my statement of opposition is basically that Mr. Linehan resigned and he did not retire." "

The granting of an order for discovery by the master of the High Court on May 11, 1990, had dispelled the prospect of a fast superficial disposition of the case. Accordingly, compliance with discovery was partial, forced and phased between July and November, 1990.

U.C.C. was in open contempt of the order for discovery at several stages in 1989. Four separate applications were necessary between July and November, 1989, in order to secure partial discovery and production of documents. Michael Enright, U.C.C. solicitor for much of the period, subsequently admitted non-compliance with discovery in a sworn affidavit dated July 22, 1991.

"Thereafter I accept, that we were in default in furnishing an Affidavit for Discovery ...."

In November, 1990, after a date for hearing had been set for February, 1991, a substantial volume of documentation was discovered in a jumbled form. None of the documentation referred to Harvard. Moreover, it was released when unlikely to be of benefit. A letter dated November 23, 1990, from Michael Enright, U.C.C. solicitor, to Edmund Hogan, my solicitor at the time, clearly indicated the fabian tactics carried forward by the universities into the High Court.

"Dear Sir,

We refer to your letter of 23rd November. We require a letter consenting to the filing of the Affidavit which we sent you this morning....

In so far as the President's file is concerned, we are preparing a supplemental Affidavit of Discovery and when this is ready we will then ask you for a letter consenting to the late filing of this Affidavit ....

We cannot and do not accept that the delay in locating the President's file has in any way affected the process of your client's claim ...."

I came on record as solicitor at that time, and obtained an adjournment of the hearing to October, 1991.

That a cover-up was in train became explicit in correspondence during Autumn and Winter, 1990 and 1991.

Enright's denial of an attempted cover-up in reply was obviously feeble and awkward. It was contained in a letter to me dated January 20, 1991:-

"We refute absolutely that any cover-up as referred to in the third last and penultimate paragraphs of your letters has taken place and no computer record ...."

The pension case, with its extensive pleadings on natural and constitutional justice, had put the focus where it belonged, i.e., on a corrupt finance committee, acting in league with their Harvard counterparts. An unsuccessful application to cull the natural and constitutional justice elements from the pension case was made on July 23, 1991. Donal O'Donnell represented university interests in court at this time.

Neither U.C.C. nor Harvard insider administrators wished the High Court to consider the critical Harvard dimension that was both proved and indicated by the affidavits and exhibits put on record between March and July, 1991. Thus, in his affidavit dated July 22, 1991, Michael Enright, U.C.C. solicitor, averred as follows:-

"It seems clear, however, that oral evidence is necessary to determine the issue in the case, and indeed in July 1991, Mr. Justice Johnson so indicated."

Notwithstanding that averment, at the hearing, U.C.C. called no witnesses.

Having applied for an oral hearing in order to circumvent the affidavit evidence, Sean O'Leary, U.C.C. counsel, subsequently sought to limit the adduction of evidence through testimony.

"Mr. O'Leary

"My Lord, I am greatly alarmed by the fact that Mr. Linehan says that he has another 30 witnesses."

Mr. Justice Barron

"We will see what happens when they come, I have had ...."

The spurious nature of the defence of the pension case became evident even in the High Court testimony of senior university administrators. Thus, it was admitted that I had been eligible for the pension claimed.

Mr. Mortell

"Yes, that was talking about strictly - that was one of the three options as I heard the judge say, that was put to you before any settlement had taken place." "

Whereas Michael Mortell's testimony established the entitlement aspect of the case, Michael Kelleher's testimony established the natural and constitutional justice aspect. He testified that he had circulated the finance committee only with facts pertaining to the period from 1987, i.e., after the abuse at Harvard and after my employment with U.C.C. had ended.

U.C.C. administrators were prepared to go to extreme lengths, even during the hearing, to cover up the abuse at Harvard. Cyril Deasy, U.C.C. deputy finance officer, swore an affidavit dated July 22, 1991, that was on record in which he averred as follows:

"Mr. Linehan then went to study in Harvard University in the United States, and as appears from some of the documentation exhibited and referred to in his Affidavit, he apparently had considerable difficulties there ...."

Deasy subsequently denied having made that affidavit during his High Court testimony on December 4, 1991:-

Appellant

"Mr. Deasy, did you make an Affidavit in the course of these proceedings?"

Mr. Deasy

"No, My Lord."
Mr. Justice Barron
"You did, did you?"
Mr. Deasy
"I don't recall making an Affidavit, no."

Thus, on July 22, 1991, Cyril Deasy swore an affidavit before a commissioner for oaths. On December 4, 1991, while under oath in the High Court, he swore that he had not sworn the affidavit.

14 Decision of Irish Supreme Court

The preparations for the Supreme Court hearing began immediately after it was decided to appeal the judgment and order of Justice Barron of the High Court dated January 31, 1992.

In the ordinary course, the appeal would not have been heard for up to two years. A motion to set an early date was made in February, 1992. At the hearing, the Chief Justice, Thomas Finlay suggested that the motion be brought again in April, 1992, when such applications were being considered. Further resort to the Supreme Court was thus needed in April, 1992. On that application, the Chief Justice set down the appeal for hearing on July 9, 1992.

The Supreme Court panel that heard the appeal comprised the since deceased Justice Niall McCarthy, Justice Seamus Egan and Justice Hugh O'Flaherty.

The appeal was to be among the last heard by Justice Niall McCarthy. On October 1, 1992, Mr. Justice McCarthy, and his wife, died tragically in a traffic collision in Spain. He was generally regarded as an outstanding defender of civil liberties and of constitutional and human rights.

The Supreme Court, even prior to the formal appeal hearing, had some knowledge of the case. Thus, first, the elements of the case and the appeal were delineated in the notice of appeal. In setting out the grounds of the appeal, this document must in some degree at least furnish a précis of the case.

Secondly, the application for an early hearing made in February and April, 1992, were accompanied by documentation that provided information about the case.

Thirdly, by reason of a most extraordinary coincidence, the personal injuries case against Harvard and U.C.C. came for adjudication in one respect before the Supreme Court on June 19, 1992. The statistical odds in favour of both related cases coming before the Supreme Court within a period of less than three weeks were astronomical – the personal injuries case came before the Supreme Court on June 19, 1992, and the appeal in the pension case came before the court on July 9, 1992.

The personal injuries case came before the Supreme Court on a refusal by the High Court to permit service of a summons outside the jurisdiction on Harvard. In affirming the High Court judgment, the implicit rationale was that the personal injuries case against Harvard should be proved in Massachusetts rather than Ireland.

A fourth means whereby the Supreme Court that heard the appeal on July 9, 1992, had prior knowledge of the case was by dint of an extensive document submitted to it prior to the hearing. This document consisted of about one thousand, two hundred and thirty four pages. Entitled *Written Submission to the Supreme Court*, it formally cited Harvard university as a major interest party in the pension case.

The oral argument in the appeal lasted only about thirty minutes. When I began to open the appeal, the late Mr. Justice N. McCarthy intervened. He asked me if I had *additional* submissions to make over and beyond those contained in the document entitled *Written Submission to the Supreme Court.* I replied in the negative. I offered however to outline the main facets of the appeal as contained in that document. Having been assured that such an oral presentation would not *add* to the material in the Written Submission, Mr. Justice McCarthy suggested that I sit down.

He then invited Sean O'Leary to argue on behalf of U.C.C., with Harvard. Mr. O'Leary spoke for perhaps ten to fifteen minutes.

After Sean O'Leary sat down, I arose in order to reply. It was pointed out to me that I could speak only to matters raised in Sean O'Leary's submission. At that point, no new lines of argument or submission could be made. When I mentioned that I had noted about twenty points made by O'Leary, and that it was my intention to take cause with about half of those, the late Mr. Justice McCarthy intervened. He stated that it would not prejudice my case if I did not speak further.

The appeal was over within about forty five minutes of its commencement. The die was cast in what has in the meantime been suggested to have been the shortest appeal in a civil case before the Irish Supreme Court.

The Supreme Court, that had commenced to hear the appeal at 11a.m., recessed at about 11.45a.m. An indication was given that the judgment would be delivered immediately after the recess.

The Supreme Court judgment, that had been delivered orally, was later reduced to writing. After reciting the pleadings, the written judgment contains the following operative parts:

" *IT IS ORDERED AND ADJUDGED that the said Appeal be allowed and that the said Judgment and Order of the High Court be set aside and discharged*

AND THIS COURT BOTH DECLARE that the Applicant in his capacity as employed on the staff of University College Cork came within the terms of Statute 79 of the Statutes of the National University of Ireland and is entitled as from the date of his retirement to a pension in accordance with the measure to be applied under that Statute.

AND IT IS ORDERED that the Respondent do pay to the Applicant his costs (limited to expenses and outlay properly incurred) of the proceedings in the High Court and of this Appeal when taxed and ascertained."

The Supreme Court judgment had vital implications for the parties as well as Harvard University.

The most obvious implication was that I would obtain my pension and costs - I would be in funds to maintain myself and my home, to establish a new life independent of an environment that I had come to loathe and, also, I would be in funds to pursue the personal injuries litigation against both U.C.C. and Harvard.

Implicit in the judgment was a strong indictment against U.C.C. administrators - although certified as *totally unfit to work* in the last months of my U.C.C. employment as a result of retaliatory abuse at Harvard in 1987, these had unlawfully withheld my pension for five years in an effort to effect a cover-up.

A period of elation and euphoria followed on the decision of the Supreme Court. Nurse Maire Clear, who had been a close and supportive friend since 1990, joined me in a random drive around the Dublin suburbs in the immediate aftermath of the judgment as we sought to absorb and savour the moment.

In the weeks following the Supreme Court judgment, it became clear that the Harvard and U.C.C. dons had decided to frustrate the judgment of the Court to the maximum extent possible. The issue of *enforcing* the judgment arose.

The pension case had arisen from abuses within U.C.C. law department in the 1985-1986 period and, more especially, from the retaliatory abuses within the Harvard law school complex in 1987. None of the U.C.C. faction who were directly involved in the earlier episode had ever appeared in court between 1986 and 1992. Moreover, the Supreme Court judgment of July 9, 1992, did not affect them financially. In other words, in personal terms, the defeat of U.C.C. in the Supreme Court had cost nothing to the individuals who were waging the war. The same was true to an even greater extent for the Harvard law dons. It is hardly surprising therefore that there was no ready compliance with the judgment.

Accordingly, I applied again to the Supreme Court on July 31, 1992, to enforce its judgment. That was the last day of sittings before the recess began in August. On this occasion, the Supreme Court refused to enforce the judgment on the basis that the application was premature. That did not make sense to me – my pension had been withheld for more than *five* years.

At this point, I petitioned about two hundred and twenty members of the Irish parliament by circular letter. U.C.C. is substantially funded by the state and, shortly after the petition, the more than five years of pension arrears that was recognised to have been owed under the Supreme Court judgment was paid.

The matter of costs payable under that judgment was still however outstanding. Expenses and outlay, that had been awarded by the Supreme Court, amounted to almost £1/4 million.

15 Financial Costs of Victory

Harvard and U.C.C. had formidable legal resources to draw on when a joint cover-up was resolved on after the abuse and injuries sustained within Harvard in 1987. The resources of Harvard law school were available. The resources of U.C.C. law faculty were also available. The latter included several members who had either direct links with events between 1985 and 1987, or who were graduates of Harvard law school. Thus, Bryan McMahon, John White and Gerard Quinn were Harvard graduates. Patrick Horgan had played a part in the events that led to my successful case against U.C.C. in 1986, and had also contributed to the universities' defence after the retaliatory abuse at Harvard in 1987.

Although none appeared in court, the interested or con-
scripted members of Harvard and U.C.C. law faculties were
the real architects of the universities' legal defence after
1987. Harvard law school, in particular, included members
with formidable credentials in litigation management.
These included Archibald Cox, who had acted as special
prosecutor in the Watergate scandal that led to the resignation of Richard Nixon. They also included Alan Dershowitz
who has defended such high profile clients as Van Bulow
and O.J. Simpson. It is only by considering the calibre of the
defence teams at their disposal that one can fully appreciate
both the ingenuity and the audacity of the universities' litigation strategy after 1987. The reports from Malden Hospital, Massachusetts, of May 10 and 11, 1987, constituted
the proverbial *smoking gun.* The universities' legal defence
work had sought to negate this by a studied and potent
cocktail of evasion, fabrication, chicanery and penguin
speak, as well as by a prolonged exercise in ventriloquism
effected through a large contingent of outside lawyers.

In the litigation after 1987 in the Irish and American
courts, Harvard was principally represented through the
legal counsel's office of Harvard, and U.C.C. was principally represented through Ronan Daly Jermyn, solicitors.
For strategic or tactical reasons, some of the legal work was
farmed out to other law offices. For instance, in the 1987-
1988 period, Harvard's defensive posture was promoted
by Tillinghast, Collins & Graham, and by Stephen J. Fortunato, Jr., two firms in Rhode Island.

In 1991, after a defamation action was commenced as
a result of the report of Dr. M. Murphy of October 3, 1989,
the legal defence work was undertaken by A. Cox & Co.,
solicitors, a firm that had unique links to Harvard.

After several months of thorough and professional investigation, the costs incurred by me pertaining to the case in
the period July, 1987, to July, 1992, were professionally cer-

tified at £210,871.84. The certificate is as follows:

"Grand total of 66 items of
Bill of Costs   £210,871.84
Accountant's Certificate
I, John Fehily, Accountant, of Rearour, Aherla
Co. Cork, hereby certify that I have verified the above
figures where vouchers make same possible. I have also
utilised affidavits, verbal communications and inspec-
tion of documents in order to corroborate the figures.
Signed: *J. Fehily*
Date: February 27, 1993

*"The Applicant in this action had sustained personal injuries
in 1987 in the last months of his 13 years of employment
with the Respondent while at Harvard University."*

The figure of £210,871.84 did not include any element
of a professional fee for me, since the Supreme Court costs
order had not provided for same.

From Item 46 of the bill of costs, it is clear that U.C.C.,
in liaison with Harvard, had contested the small pension
in Cork District Court between 1987 and 1989. It had also
contested the pension before eight judges of the High
Court between 1990 and 1992 - i.e., Justices Lavan, Johnson, Hamilton, Lardner, Lynch, Morris, Murphy and Barron. It had likewise contested the pension before the master of the High Court. In the context of the appeal to the
Supreme Court, U.C.C. in liaison with Harvard, at different stages contested the pension before the late Justice N.
McCarthy, Chief Justice Finlay and also Justices O'Flaherty and Egan. In other words, a pension that in 1987 was
worth about £125.00 net per week was contested before
fourteen judges of the Irish courts. That figure of fourteen
does not include the two taxing masters who were later to
engage in the charade in the taxing master's office.

The prolonged litigation had suited U.C.C. and Harvard for several reasons. First, the costs of running the litigation were insignificant relative to the wealth of both universities. Time Magazine did a special feature on Harvard on its three hundred and fiftieth anniversary in 1986. At that time, the university had a $3.5 billion dollar endowment and a $650 million dollar annual budget. U.C.C. is also a wealthy institution, not least because of its substantial subvention by the Irish state. Its total assets are about £100 million, and it has an annual income of more than £66 million in the current year.

In contrast, following the abuse and injuries sustained within Harvard in 1987, I was unable to engage in full-time employment. After I had ceased part-time consultancy in 1989, I had no income whatsoever. My financial circumstances were a second obvious reason why it suited Harvard and U.C.C. to prolong the pension case.

The pension claimed in the case was worth only about £145 net weekly, even in 1992 at the time of the Supreme Court judgment. However, it had by July, 1994, cost me and those who supported me in the case over £290,000 to secure the pension.

The sum of about £290,000 costs of succeeding in the Supreme Court is made up of some £210,000 costs of prosecuting the case, £30,000 loss of interest on the costs between July, 1992, and July, 1993, and £20,000 costs of preparation and presentation at the taxation of costs between July, 1992, and July, 1993. All these figures are independently and professionally proved and certified.

U.C.C., in liaison with Harvard, incurred at least equivalent costs. In fact, because their expenses and outlay were incurred at civil service rates, and with the equivalent of civil service overheads, the university costs would also have exceeded £$^1/_2$ million in real terms.

If one adds the costs of the more than thirty two state employees who participated in the adjudication – judges, taxing masters, registrars, tipstaffs, clerks and so forth – one arrives at a somewhat startling conclusion. That is that, at open market rates, well over £1 million costs were incurred between 1987 and 1994 in defending and adjudicating on a small pension case.

This projection of university costs does not include legal professional fees. The addition of same was likely to have pushed the cost of the universities' bill to well over £1 million. This figure involves imputing minimal professional fees, not for the entire cadre of the Harvard and U.C.C. legal defence team, but only for those outside lawyers used to front the defence in the Irish courts between 1987 and 1993. This team included Frank Daly, Michael Enright and Richard Martin, of Ronan, Daly, Jermyn, solicitors. It included Pearts and Co., solicitors and town agents. It also included Patricia Lord, solicitor and legal costs accountant. Among the string of counsel who had acted in court were Donal O'Donnell and Sean O'Leary. Moreover, on the assumption that U.C.C. had not changed its senior counsel after the 1986 High Court case, the external defence team also included Dermot Gleeson.

The imputation of professional fees of only £1/2 million in respect of this front team for the seven years involved is ultra conservative. That can be demonstrated by reference to the fee rates known to be charged by certain of them. Thus, in 1995, Dermot Gleeson and Donal O'Donnell presented bills of £1.1 million and £990,000.00, respectively, for their work in the Beef Tribunal that had run for some eighteen months. These bills involved fee rates of between £1,000.00 and £3,000.00 per day.

Realistically, the floor figure for the universities' legal costs between 1987 and 1993 is likely to have been far in excess of £1 million. The combined wealth of Harvard and U.C.C. was the quintessential honeypot, and the financial interests of the intermediaries are a key factor in understanding the course of the attempted cover-up that began in 1987.

Apart from the lawyers and fixers who have been paid off in the scandal, the only completely clear beneficiary to date is Harvard.

As will be seen in greater detail later, it became clear shortly after the late Tom O'Connor sat as taxing master in the matter of costs on February 1, 1993, that the process

was politically rigged against me and those who supported me in the case.

16 Effective Reversal of Irish Supreme Court Order

Charles Haughey was prime minister between February,
1987, and February, 1992. As such, he had considerable
influence over the management of U.C.C., and close contacts with its senior administrators.

Referred to while prime minister as *The Boss* by his cabinet colleagues, Haughey's entire political career had been
controversial. He was indicted in 1970 for an alleged
attempt to import arms illegally into the state while minister for finance. He denied the charge and was acquitted
by a jury, although his evidence had been contradicted by
that of several of his co-accused. Justice Henchy, presiding, stated that he:-

*"would like to be able to suggest some way you can avoid
holding there is perjury in this case."*

Twenty-seven years later, on February 8, 1997, Kevin
Boland, Haughey's former government colleague and
political ally, stated that Haughey had been mistaken in
1970 when he denied knowledge of an attempt to import
arms. Boland claimed that Haughey had briefed him in his
ministerial office on the planned importation.

Charles Haughey became prime minister for the first
time in March, 1982. His government was defeated in a
general election nine months later. Shortly thereafter, it
was revealed that one of his ministers, Sean Doherty, while
in office, had instructed the police to tap the telephones of
two political journalists, Bruce Arnold and Geraldine
Kennedy. In a separate disclosure, it was revealed that a
second minister, Ray MacSharry, had used a police tape to
bug a conversation with another ministerial colleague,
Martin O'Donoghue. The transcript of the bugged con-

versation reads in part as follows:-

M. O'Donoghue

"I think in fairness what was said there was that I don't think what anyone was implying that there was any substance to it. After all I am supposed to have been paid £50,000 for behaving the way I did in February, but I know how true that is. What was being said was if there was any suggestion of somebody being compromised financially that it would be sorted out. But the money thing that I heard about around town was that the boss was in financial trouble and certainly again if that was one of the problems it would be better to organise some way of financing it."

R. MacSharry

"For Haughey to be in trouble, I mean he has such... he could not be in trouble."

M. O'Donoghue

"Is there not that persistent story around town, you know that there is pressure on him to get...development from Baldoyle up because it is worth all that much."

R. MacSharry

"You know yourself that the story goes on about every Fianna Fail politician...."

Several resignations followed shortly after the telephone tapping and bugging disclosures. Martin O'Donoghue, then an economics professor at Trinity College, Dublin, resigned the Fianna Fail party whip. So did Sean Doherty. The police commissioner, Patrick McLoughlin, and deputy commissioner, Joe Ainsworth, also resigned.

Charles Haughey, however, survived a motion demanding that he resign as leader of the Fianna Fail party. That was notwithstanding that the disclosures had fuelled rumours that his personal finances were troubled, and that he stood to gain if planning permission were given for a highly controversial housing development in North Dublin.

He had denied both involvement in and knowledge of either the telephone tapping or the bugging while prime minister.

Ten years later, in January 1992, Sean Doherty precipitated Haughey's eventual retirement from party politics, by stating that, in 1982, he had given transcripts of the tapped telephone conversations to Haughey while he was prime minister.

Kennedy, Arnold and the latter's wife, Mavis, sued the state for breach of their rights to privacy and free expression. They won a total of £50,000.

It has recently been revealed that Kennedy and Arnold were not the only journalists being tapped in 1982. In March, 1997, Vincent Browne disclosed that his telephone had been tapped between 1975 and 1983 by successive governments. His action against the state for breach of his constitutional rights was eventually settled only in 1995. He received £91,000 and costs of about £100,000.

U.C.C. is substantially funded by the state. Thus, for instance, student fees are paid by the state. The government nominates two members to its governing body. A practice of monthly meetings between the prime minister and university presidents exists. There is considerable interactivity between state and university personnel on an ongoing basis.

Charles Haughey's second term as prime minister between 1987 and 1992 virtually coincided with the period when the U.C.C. and Harvard cover-up attempts were most successful. The universities refused in 1987 and thereafter to pay compensation for the injuries inflicted at Harvard. U.C.C. also unlawfully withheld my pension in 1987, and engaged in a prolonged and obscene defence of its position until the Supreme Court decision of July 9, 1992.

It is implausible that Charles Haughey, as prime minister, had not known of and condoned the ruthless, grotesque and extended actions effected by U.C.C. and Harvard in pursuance of a cover-up after 1987. Moreover, a pattern of other hostile actions by state agencies emerged after 1987. Thus, for instance, the revenue commissioners wrongfully withheld a substantial tax refund owed me that I recovered only by court action in 1990.

Again, the state resorted to outright fiction when I sued the department of foreign affairs for failing to assist me while at Harvard. The defence by the chief state solicitor's office included a claim that I had not been at Harvard during the 1986-1987 academic year. Moreover, the extraordinary decision of the High Court in the pension case against U.C.C., with Harvard, was delivered on January 31, 1992 - that was indeed only five days before C.J. Haughey was eventually replaced as leader of Fianna Fail by Albert Reynolds.

In sum, the die had been cast long before the strange happenings in the taxing master's office in 1993, when a middle ranking civil servant purported to reverse a Supreme Court costs order. Coordination of state agencies in furtherance of policy is commonplace. Ample evidence of such in my regard emerged during Haughey's final stint as prime minister.

The functions of the taxing master's office are essentially administrative. The office is not a court and it became clear on February 1, 1993, that the taxation of costs had been rigged so as to reverse the Supreme Court order. This was an ultimate abuse of the legal system.

Nurse Maire Clear is one of the indirect beneficiaries under the Supreme Court order for costs. She had been a major contributor in a practical and financial way in the litigation between 1990 and 1992. She also was one of eight witnesses who attended on the first attempted taxation of costs on February 1, 1993. Her dismay and justified anger at those proceedings, as well as her interest in recovering her money, stimulated her to writing the following account of what transpired.

"Quest for Justice
Today, February 1, 1993, was the day the Expenses and Out-

lay were to be decided by a Taxing-Master of the High Court. Those of us who worked so hard and so patiently for this case, all small, ordinary people of little means and much dedication and goodwill, would be repaid Today.

We were all in debt owing to the Case, but David had beaten Goliath and the highest Court in the land had ordered that David be recompensed for the mountains of typing, photocopying, binding, the telephoning, train-fares, accommodation, etc., for most of which up-front money had been required. My happy thought was that my Bank Loan would be repaid. (One of the people present, at the Taxation, who is owed a substantial sum arising from the Supreme Court Order, and who has a small struggling business, went to jail for six days recently because he could not find £2,000 demanded by a major Bank).

The Taxing-Master took his seat. He immediately complained about the format of the Bill presented to him by Denis. Denis pointed out politely that the guidelines for the format had come from a Registrar at the Taxing-Master's own office.

The Master then proceeded to ignore the Supreme Court Order, demanding a copy of the High Court Order, even though it was irrelevant, having been set aside and over-ruled. He threatened not to proceed without this apparently vital document. He listened at length to the U.C.C. representative as she quoted uncomplimentary comments from the over-ruled Judge. When Denis got a chance to reply, he was to be rudely interrupted after a few minutes and prevented from having a proper hearing - his right in Law.

The Master complained again. 'I have a figure here for £37,500' he said - and went on about 'a rigmarole' which was following it. (A breakdown of the figures). He complained about the Bill for binding, commenting that he had never seen it (binding) presented on a Bill before. (If that is so, I wonder, who pays for it? Documents have to be bound before being presented to a Judge). Behind me, the printer/Binder, who had travelled from Cork exclaimed audibly in surprise.

The Taxing-Master complained about the necessity of

employing a Stenographer in the High Court. (Yet the Supreme Court requires a Transcript of Evidence before hearing an Appeal).

The little group of us moved uneasily in our seats and exchanged glances. This procedure was simply getting 'curiouser and curiouser.'

The Master complained again. 'I have no breakdown for this figure for £37,500' he said (what about 'the rigmarole?'). He was immediately handed another - more detailed - breakdown - and refused it. 'If it's not in front of me I haven't got it' he said, like a character from Alice in Wonderland. After another few verbal tos and fros he drew his pen across it. 'Part 1, £37,500 - I'm disallowing it' he stated. There was a horrified gasp from our group. Much of the General Expenses were in there.

Denis protested loudly, pointing out that the Supreme Court specifically stated that the Expenses of taking the case to court were to be awarded. 'It's disallowed' growled the Taxing-Master. There was a shocked silence. I began to experience an air of unreality. Was the Supreme Court Order, then, as useless as an out-of-date bus ticket?

Denis was slowly closing his books as the coup-de-grace was delivered from the bench. 'Dress-hire' said the Master slowly, with an air of mockery. 'What was that for, a tuxedo or something?' I felt anger rise within me. Denis did not have a suit proper for court-wear. Out of respect for the Court, he hired the proper attire.

These proceedings were getting farcical. Denis asked for leave to confer. Outside the door, we decided that the only option was to withdraw the Bill and present it at a later date, before either the Court or the other Taxing-Master.

We returned to Cork. We had come expecting Justice, we left stunned and disillusioned. If we had cherished before in our hearts a sense of trust in, and national pride for, the Irish seat of Justice, the Four Courts, this trust was collapsing like a house of cards. For it seemed that, judging by today's performance, black could be made white and white black, the

High Court has more clout than the Supreme Court, and the winner is really the loser. The Supreme Court Case was won on July 9th last, and here we are, eight months later, still fighting, still typing, still binding, still travelling, still spending ...."

The U.C.C. representative referred to in Maire Clear's article was Patricia Lord, solicitor. The vehemence and occasional stridency that she brought to her role was indicative of the substantial fees that participants in the attempted cover-up have received.

The taxing master referred to in Miss Clear's article was the late Tom O'Connor. A former election agent of C. J. Haughey, Mr. O'Connor made clear on February 1, 1993, that he was reversing the Supreme Court Order as to costs. Tom O'Connor was a brother of *Pat O'Connor Pat O'Connor,* so nicknamed because of a charge of double voting against him in 1982 when he was Charles Haughey's election agent. Although the prosecution proved that he had applied for ballot papers in two polling stations, the charge was dismissed on the ground that it was legally impossible to prove that a person had voted even once.

Shortly after I was injured at Harvard in 1987, Haughey had visited that university in April, 1988, on foot of an invitation extended through the department of foreign affairs. The invitation had caused me disquiet even then. The range of hostile actions against me by the Irish state thereafter fed my suspicions that Haughey had been recruited as a political helmsman in the cover-up. The links between Tom O'Connor and Haughey, and the primal steal in the taxing master's office on February 1, 1993, confirmed those suspicions.

We refused to deal further with Tom O'Connor in the taxing master's office, but arranged for a resumption of the attempted taxation under the only other taxing master, James Flynn. Flynn had a similar political pedigree to Tom O'Connor, having been appointed by Albert Reynolds who had succeeded Charles Haughey as prime minister. He was appointed taxing master on October 21, 1992, just over three months after the Supreme Court order against U.C.C., with Harvard.

A second attempt at a taxation of costs was made on April 26, 1993. This second attempt was adjourned after one day with only about five of the sixty four items on the bill of costs being ruled on. James Flynn made two obviously invalid rulings at the outset, that had the effects of effectively disallowing all costs in the District Court between 1987 and 1989, and the costs of the interlocutory proceedings in the High Court between 1990 and 1991.

John Fehily, accountant, was one of those who witnessed the repeated continuation of the abuse of office on April 26, 1993. In an affidavit to the High Court dated July 1, 1993, Mr. Fehily had the following observations to make:

"6.These Rulings by Master Flynn had a major negative impact on the vouched and proved Costs claimed, which are in excess of £210,000. It effectively excluded the Costs over three and a half years of the proceedings that had been ongoing for five years culminating in the Supreme Court Judgment of July 9, 1992.

7. Further, during this April session, only six Items were adjudicated on by Master Flynn. These items amounted to over £14,600, but, less than £600 was allowed. This represented a Disallowance of about 96% on Costs that were fully proved and the allowance of which was fully supported by legal principles."

Certain of the beneficiaries under the Supreme Court costs order refused to participate in the masquerade in the taxing master's office after April 26, 1993.

It had become evident by April 26, 1993, to all beneficiaries under the Supreme Court order of July 9, 1992, that the order was being dishonoured within the taxing master's office, that is less than half a mile from the Supreme Court.

As it subsequently became clear, the political rigging of the costs also extended into the highest levels of the judiciary.

17 Judicial Blind Eye

After the repeat debacle in the taxing master's office on April 26, 1993, a further enforcement-type application was made to the Supreme Court on June 9, 1993. This was the fourth such application since it had made its judgment in the case on July 9, 1992. Previous enforcement-type applications had been made on July 31, 1992, January 22, 1993, and March 5, 1993. All of these had been to no avail. Notwithstanding the refusal of, first, U.C.C. and, secondly, the taxing master's office, to give effect to the costs order, the Supreme Court had not been prepared to intervene.

The Supreme Court, like all courts, has an inherent jurisdiction in contempt. The costs order had repeatedly been treated with contempt during the previous eleven months, to my detriment, and that of the other beneficiaries as well as our families. It was long-overdue that the court should intervene and stand over its own order.

It had been brought to my attention that grounds for disqualification existed in relation to one of the judges who had sat on the Supreme Court panel that had been adjudicating on the enforcement-type applications. Justice Hugh O'Flaherty was the justice in question. He had been appointed to the Supreme Court in 1990 by Charles Haughey.

The Supreme Court panel that heard the enforcement-type application on June 9, 1992, remained unchanged since the previous application. That panel consisted of Justices O'Flaherty, Egan and Denham. Justice O'Flaherty was again presiding on June 9, 1993. I indicated in a diplomatic manner that I had two grounds of objection to one member of the court. This gave Justice O'Flaherty the opportunity to disqualify himself with tact, and without my mentioning his links with either the academic legal world or the McMahon family. He did not take that opportunity. Having indicated that the court had anticipated certain objections, Justice O'Flaherty denied me the right to object to his sitting. He also refused my application.

Moreover, he purported to bar me from the Supreme Court in relation to the case. The terms of the order read as follows:-

"... The Court declines to entertain the said Motions on the grounds that it has no jurisdiction to entertain them... and directs that no further Motions be accepted from the Applicant in this matter."

I was being denied access to the Supreme Court to enforce payment of a sum of over £^{1}/$_4$ million, including interest, then owed me under a Supreme Court order made eleven months previously.

Thus, the Supreme Court, while not reversing its costs order of July 9, 1992, clearly signalled that it was not standing over it.

The signals given by the Supreme Court on June 9, 1993, had not been lost on James Flynn when a further attempt at effecting a taxation resumed on June 10, 1993. Following is an abbreviated extract from the joint affidavit of myself, Patrick O'Leary, Michael Grimes and Maire Clear dated July 1, 1993.

"47. Master Flynn in general failed to give reasons for the Rulings that disallowed nearly 90% of the £147,000 of Claims that were adjudicated on....

48. Secondly, Master Flynn, likewise, generally refused to cite authorities for his virtually unbroken stream of disallowance Rulings. At one point, he made the telling and astonishing observation that he "did not need any authority"............. "

Neither the indirect claimants under the costs order, nor the accountant, were prepared to attend the charade in the taxing master's office after June 11, 1993.

A further application to the High Court was made on July 12, 1993. This sought a variety of remedies, including annulment of the proceedings in the taxing master's office, and directions in relation to the conduct of the taxation.

The High Court application of July 12, 1993, came before Judge Lavan. He refused all remedies in a summary manner. Lavan had been appointed to the High Court by Charles Haughey in 1989.

The constitutional doctrine of separation of powers is not always realised in practice. This was a factor in November, 1996, when responsibility for the courts was transferred from the department of justice to an independent authority. An Irish Times editorial on November 12, 1996, summed up the regime that had prevailed:-

"... Senior judges have long sought a special agency to take on the running of the courts.

Governments of every hue have refused to respond... The politicians have preferred to keep a tight control... on the judiciary."

Each of the four officials who had refused to enforce the Supreme Court costs order of July 9, 1992 - O'Connor, Flynn, O'Flaherty and Lavan - owed their positions either to Charles Haughey or to his party. That could be a remarkable coincidence. I do not believe that it is.

18 Department of Justice

By public letter of petition dated September 25, 1993, forwarded to a number of politicians, I set out the abuses of the taxing master's office that had been taking place in the interests of U.C.C. and Harvard.

As a result of that letter, acknowledgments or representations were made by several members of the Irish parliament. Both Robert Molloy and Pat Cox of the Progressive Democrats received replies to their representations to the Taxing Master's Office that they in turn communicated to me. These replies were by Brendan Minnock, chief clerk.

His letters contained the following identical quotations:-
".... in the taxation of this Bill, there has been no attempt to

*reverse [the Supreme Court] Order or to deny due process
to Mr. Linehan ....*

*Master Flynn has at all times acted fairly and objective-
ly in the course of his duties concerning this taxation and
has offered every facility to Mr. Linehan and he assures you
that he intends to adopt this approach until the matter is
finalised ...."*

The initial stage of the taxation of costs was concluded on
November 23, 1993. James Flynn refused to give his rulings on that date. This necessitated a further trip to Dublin
on December 8, 1993.

Since the Supreme Court Order had been made on July
9, 1992, over ten separate trips to Dublin had been necessitated to arrange and present at the attempted taxation of
costs. A van had been hired on several occasions to carry
the proofs of costs on the return journey between Cork and
Dublin. Hotel expenses for up to four of the beneficiaries
under the costs order and their representatives had been
incurred. Moreover, there was no reimbursement for the
time, expenses or work done in relation to same. U.C.C.
and Harvard were obviously gaining by this process. I was
obviously losing.

On December 8, 1993, James Flynn was noticeably ill as
he delivered his remaining rulings in the initial stage of
taxation. His reading of same was interrupted and
adjourned for over an hour. These rulings purported to dis-
allow the fees of the town agent cum legal executive, the
costs of the twenty one trips of attending the case in Dublin,
suit hire, office utilities, nursing expenses, library expenses, twenty of the twenty-two *viaticum* paid to witnesses,
and all professional witness expenses except those of two
U.C.C. medical affiliates – about twenty three witnesses
had testified out of more than fifty who had been summoned. The rulings disallowed the expenses and outlay in
respect of all medical proofs – a finding that must rank as
one of the most perverse in legal history. Also disallowed

was loan interest incurred in the presentation of the case. Only £250 was allowed in respect of certified costs of more than £7,000 for telephone, postage and incidentals over the five year duration of the case between July, 1987 and July, 1992.

The rulings gave the lie to the notion of a judicial and legal system operating within the framework of a constitutional democracy.

After Flynn had given his rulings on December 8, 1993, I verbally requested an interim certificate for the costs that had then been allowed. That was not available at that time. Further calculations were needed, and special deployment of staff to prepare the certificate would be necessary. Stamp duty of over £300.00 would be needed to take up the certificate. Because the conduct of the taxation was in my name, I would need to attend personally in the taxing master's office in Dublin on yet another occasion.

At that stage, the extraordinary suggestion was made that the matter could be expedited by proceeding on the basis that costs had been agreed between me and U.C.C.! Brendan Minnock, clerk, pointed out that no stamp duty would then be payable, no interim certificate would be necessary and U.C.C. might agree to *pay* quickly.

I realised that the suggestion had been made, not in my interests, but in the interests of the universities, the taxing master's office, and the civil service and political controllers behind the scenes. If a document were compiled stating that *costs had been agreed*, the sham exercise that had occurred within the taxing master's office between February 1 and December 8, 1993, could have been discounted for record, legal and financial purposes as having been inconclusive. No official within the department of justice would have been responsible for disallowing about 98% of my proved costs.

At that time, Tim Dalton was the secretary of the department of justice. Like Hugh O'Flaherty on the Supreme Court, Tim Dalton hailed from Kerry. Tim Dalton would have in turn been answerable to the minister for justice. At that time, in 1993, Maire Geoghegan-Quinn held that office.

In terms of legal theory, the senior official of a department has *prima facie* responsibility in some degree for the actions of lower-ranking officials in that department.

I returned once again to the taxing master's office on December 10, 1993, to take up the interim certificate of taxation for the £6,137.82 of the costs that had been allowed. This represented less than 3% of the proved costs of the litigation as certified by the accountant who had prepared the bill of costs.

A professional photographer accompanied me.

The interim certificate was not ready. Moreover, it would not be furnished unless and until I paid over £300.00 stamp duty. Also, certain vouchers needed to be produced – I had not been informed of this requirement previously but, fortunately, the vouchers were readily available.

James Flynn was not present in the taxing master's office to sign the interim certificate on December 10, 1993. I would need to return in the afternoon. Another entire day was thus wasted in collecting slightly over 2% of proved costs granted under a Supreme Court order made eighteen months previously.

Collection of the £6,137.82 due under the interim certificate of taxation occupied part of a further three days in December, 1993. Notwithstanding two personal calls to the finance office of University College Cork, direct payment was refused by that office. It required three personal calls to the office of Ronan Daly Jermyn, solicitors for the university, before payment was made.

Formal notice of objections to all disallowances made, and an application for review of the taxation, together with the grounds of objections, were filed and served by letter dated December 21, 1993 pursuant to the Superior Court rules. The grounds of objections expressly included *gross corruption and manifest bias.*

Yet another personal attendance was required on December 22, 1993, at the taxing master's office to secure a date for the review. At that application, January 31, 1994, was set as the review date.

The essential purpose of a review of taxation is to challenge decisions of a taxing master. That is impossible if the reasons for decisions have not been given. In a further attempt to enable the review of taxation to proceed as scheduled on January 31, 1994, I again wrote to the taxing master's office by letter dated January 28, 1994. No reply to that letter was made. The review of taxation set down for January 31, 1994, was rendered impossible by the taxing master's office.

Less than 3% of proved and justified costs had been sanctioned by the taxing master's office. The average allowance rate is about 83%. The shortfall in the costs that were purported to have been measured was £204,734.02. That was exclusive of the interest on the costs since July, 1992. Also, that figure does not represent the substantial costs incurred in seeking to recover these costs. Neither did it capture the further eighteen months spoliation of the creditors' lives that had been expended since the Supreme Court costs order had been made on July 9, 1992.

In practical financial terms, a purported reversal of that Supreme Court costs order had been made.

19 The Politicians

The costs misappropriated within the Irish judicial system can properly be described as:-

"[A] *mere bud on the forest tree of the parent suit.*"

This metaphor is taken from *Bleak House*, that focuses in particular on the case of *Jarndyce and Jarndyce.* Dickens introduced the case to the reader in a manner that is indicated by the following extract:-

"Jarndyce and Jarndyce has passed into a joke. That is the only good that has ever come out of it. It has been death to many, but it is a joke in the profession. Every master in Chancery has had a reference out of it. Every Chancellor was 'in it,' for somebody or other, when he was counsel at the bar .... The last Lord Chancellor handled it neatly when, correcting Mr. Blowers, the eminent silk gown who said that such a thing might happen when the sky rained potatoes, he observed, 'or when we get through Jarndyce and Jarndyce, Mr. Blowers;' –a pleasantry that particularly tickled the maces, bags and pursers.

...

Thus, in the midst of the mud and at the heart of the fog, sits the Lord High Chancellor in his High Court of Chancery.

"Mr. Tangle," says the Lord High Chancellor, latterly something restless under the eloquence of that learned gentleman.

"Mlud," says Mr. Tangle. Mr. Tangle knows more of Jarndyce and Jarndyce than anybody. He is famous for it – supposed never to have read anything else since he left school.

"Have you nearly concluded your argument?"

"Mlud, no – variety of points – feel it my duty tsubmit –ludship," is the reply that slides out of Mr. Tangle.

"Several members of the bar are still to be heard, I believe?" says the Chancellor, with a slight smile.

Eighteen of Mr. Tangle's learned friends, each armed with a little summary of eighteen hundred sheets, bob up like eighteen hammers in a pinaforte, make eighteen bows, and drop into their eighteen places of obscurity.

"We will proceed with the hearing on Wednesday fortnight," says the Chancellor.

"For the question of issue is only a question of costs, a mere bud on the forest tree of the parent suit, and really will come to a settlement one of these days." "

The chancellor's metaphorical description of the question of costs in *Jarndyce and Jarndyce* as being *a mere bud on the forest tree of the parent suit"* could be readily transplanted into the present context, in which the *forest tree of the parent suit* would be equivalent to the liability of U.C.C. and Harvard to pay very substantial compensation in respect of the abuse and personal injuries inflicted at Harvard between March and May, 1987.

In another respect, also, there is a clear parallel between Dickens' *Jarndyce and Jarndyce* and the litigation here involving U.C.C. and Harvard. In the fictional case, the litigation burgeoned and continued indefinitely in large part because of the size of the estate that was at issue. This attracted and supported innumerable attendants. In the present litigation complex, the same phenomenon – that is indeed familiar to most if not all experienced lawyers – has also been a major factor. The virtually bottomless defence budgets of U.C.C. and Harvard in combination, as well as the substantial damages claimed in the personal injuries case, have given rise to innumerable and sustained abuses by politicians, lawyers, doctors, university administrators and civil servants.

20 The Attorney General

Charles Haughey finally resigned as leader of Fianna Fail in February, 1992. Sean Doherty's statement that he had given transcripts of the tapped telephone calls to Haughey in 1982 was the catalyst. The statement challenged the crucial denials made by Haughey ten years previously.

Haughey's standing was at a low ebb in early 1992. A torrent of allegations had his involvement in or knowledge of a long series of financial scandals. Greencore, Telecom, Carysfort, Goodman, NCB and Celtic Helicopters had become household names in connection with controversial dealings in state and semi-state bodies.

Carysfort is illustrative. It involved a decision by Uni-

versity College Dublin to buy Carysfort for £8 million from
a friend of Fianna Fail who, just seven months previously, had bought it for £6.5 million. Like U.C.C., University
College Dublin is a constituent college of the national university of Ireland, and was thus within Haughey's sphere
of influence. In *Goodbye to All That*, investigative journalist
Gene Kerrigan maintained that it was common knowledge
that Haughey intervened in that affair. His political obit-
uary of Haughey is also adroit:-

*"...too many names of (Haughey's) friends, and in one case
his relative, popped up in controversial circumstances."*

It is noteworthy that Greencore, one of the companies mentioned above, was recently censured by the European
Commission for breach of european law. On May 14, 1997,
the company was fined a record £6.6 million for serious
and prolonged anti-competitive practices.

New light was shed on the finances of Charles Haughey
in the 1990 to 1992 period in March, 1997. The source is an
affidavit by Ben Dunne, one time chairman of Dunnes
Stores, Ireland's largest private company. The affidavit
was drawn in the context of the payment to politicians tribunal set up on February 7, 1997. Dunne swears that he
gifted more than £1 million to Haughey, on foot of
approaches by an accountant in 1990 and 1991 seeking
financial help. The affidavit claims that, at that time,
Haughey was in severe financial difficulty and faced the
forced sale of his 300 acre estate in north County Dublin.
At the time Haughey earned about £70,000 yearly as prime
minister and had a state pension of £35,000. These could
obviously not sustain the lifestyle he enjoyed. Apart from
his estate, he owns an island, a yacht, racehorses, a series
of smaller properties dotted throughout Ireland and a private collection of art and sculpture.
The Fianna Fáil-Labour coalition government collapsed
ignominiously in November, 1994, as a result of a different scandal that also arose within the legal system. The

political fallout included the resignations in rapid succession of two attorney generals and of the President of the High Court, an office that one of them had held for less than a week.

I wrote to the new prime minister, John Bruton, and several of the ministers in the new government by letter dated December 23, 1994. In that letter, I pointed out that:-

"I was seriously injured at Harvard University in 1987 while in employment with University College Cork ... Both universities have refused to pay compensation, although the injuries and the responsibility have been proved and admitted in both the Irish and American legal systems."

I also produced evidence of the misappropriation of costs that had occurred in the taxing master's office in 1993 in defiance of the Supreme Court order of July 9, 1992. The initial responses to my letter dated December 23, 1994, were good.

After seven and a half years, in open correspondence, at ministerial level, the issue of compensation for personal injuries arising from the abuse at Harvard in 1987 while in U.C.C. employment was expressly acknowledged. A milestone had been reached.

My letter dated December 23, 1994, had also been sent to Ms. Jean Kennedy-Smith, American ambassador to Ireland. A diplomatic reply to same dated January 4, 1995, was received from the staff of the American embassy in Dublin. This read in part that:-

"I note that you ... are requesting that the Embassy of the United States approach the other parties named in [the legal] proceedings, i.e. University College Cork and Harvard University, on your behalf ....

As you are a citizen of Ireland, I suggest that you contact the Irish Department of Foreign Affairs, who should be able to furnish the address and telephone number of the Irish Consulate General with jurisdiction over the State of Massachusetts ...."

However, several countervailing factors suggested

that the initial auguries from the new government might not reflect its ultimate position. The most important of these, arguably, was the identity of the new attorney general, Dermot Gleeson.

This appointment raised the issue of whether the new government would deal with the matter of costs and compensation in a completely fair and independent manner. Under article 30.1 of the constitution, it is provided that:-

"There shall be an Attorney General who shall be the adviser of the Government in matters of law and legal opinion .... "

Dermot Gleeson's appointment as attorney general raised issues of both actual and objective bias in relation to how he might advise the new government in relation to the litigation. At least three distinct grounds existed. First, Gleeson had lectured at U.C.C. law faculty in the 1970's.

Secondly, he had acted as senior counsel in the 1986 High Court case against U.C.C. that arose from the initial wrongdoing – therefore, professionally, he had previously taken a side in the conflict. Thirdly, it would be reasonable to assume that the new attorney general had been consulted in the context of the litigation against U.C.C. in the period of the attempted cover-up that had followed the retaliatory abuse at Harvard in 1987.

A price was put on my head in 1987, and legal and medical bounty hunters were deployed accordingly. That these had their political counterparts was confirmed by the attempted taxation of the Supreme Court costs order that began in 1993.

It became clear shortly after the inauguration of the Rainbow Coalition government in December, 1994, that the cover-up policy initiated under the Fianna Fáil government of Charles Haughey in 1987 was being endorsed by the new regime. That position is captured in letters dated January 24 and 30, 1995, from Nora Owen, and Niamh Bhreathnach, the new ministers for justice and education, respectively.

By the end of January, 1995, the colours and significance

of the new Rainbow Coalition government had come into clear focus. Assaults on a lawyer by academics would be attempted to be covered up. No compensation would be paid. A Supreme Court order that awarded costs certified at nearly £^{1}/$_4$ million would not be enforced.

These phenomena were permissible when Harvard law school was in court.

21 Ten Million Dollar Claim in American Courts

Harvard law school was in the Irish court system since 1987, as a silent partner in the pension case that was ostensibly being defended by U.C.C. The logic and the evidence fully supports that contention. Although not formally on record in the pension case, Harvard had been what is technically referred to as a privy in interest.

The cunning of the Harvard approach is self-evident. In the pension case, it was not formally at risk in a reputational sense. Neither was it at risk financially. Also, the prolongation of the pension case could provide a lapse of time such as might later be utilised as a statute of limitations defence in the personal injuries case. The pension case could be used to attempt to discredit me. Also, the litigation could be used to drain my financial resources.

The Harvard law school's plan to fight in a safe and cost-free manner behind the U.C.C. corporate veil developed shortly after the abuse and injuries inflicted within Harvard in 1987. Its inception is traceable from the correspondence of, for instance, Michael Keating in the 1987-1988 period.

While the relatively small pension case was being tortuously prolonged within the Irish legal system from 1987 onwards, the underlying personal injuries litigation was deferred. That became legally ripe for commencement only in 1992, on foot of the evidence and researches that came to fruition in the context of the appeal of the pension case to the Irish Supreme Court in July, 1992.

A complaint against Harvard for personal injuries was prepared in the following months and filed in the U.S. District Court, District of Massachusetts on December 30, 1992.

The complaint claimed about ten million dollars from Harvard in the following terms:-

"264. ....

> *In 1987, the Plaintiff's general health was good, and his physical health was excellent, prior to the abuse within Harvard University between March and May, 1987. The Plaintiff's credentials, in terms of both experience and qualifications, were excellent. At age thirty five, the Plaintiff was in the prime of his life.*

265. *In the parallel proceedings in Ireland, damages in the amount of about one and a half million pounds (1.5 million pounds) are claimed by reference to the size of awards in that jurisdiction in respect of the liability of University College Cork for the serious personal injuries inflicted between March and May, 1987.*

266. *In these proceedings, damages in the amount of about ten million dollars ($10 million) are claimed by reference to the size of awards in this jurisdiction in respect of the liability of Harvard University for the serious personal injuries inflicted between March and May, 1987 ....*

> *The grounds for the personal injuries limb of the Complaint evolved around the sonic abuse that had taken place within the Harvard Law complex in March and April, 1987. "*

The fury of senior U.C.C. administrators at having been properly discredited in the Irish High Court in 1986 had been translated into action by their Harvard counterparts. The liaison between U.C.C. and Harvard law dons and their administrative associates resulted in a mafia-type sting operation that would arouse the admiration and envy of any sophisticated gangster organisation. The physical aspect of the sting operation was partly set out in the complaint filed in the U.S. District Court as follows:

" 95   *In fact as well as in law, the contract in respect of the dormitory accommodation at Room 220, Holmes Hall, Harvard University, is one of the most important contracts. Since the personal injuries sustained by the Plaintiff between March and May, 1987, were caused by the application to him of a sonic device installed in a room adjoining the said Room 220, Holmes Hall, the said contract for accommodation establishes a contractual basis for the liability of Harvard University in respect of the personal injuries herein complained of ....*

153.   *.... The said sonic abuse is outlined in the Plaintiff's Sworn Deposition dated August 31, 1987:-*

        'The noise complained of generally was a high pitch frequency sound that over a period of time damaged my hearing and has left me with constant earaches. I first noticed the noise on Sunday evening, March 1, the same evening that I discovered my room to have been broken into. Over a period of about twenty minutes, the high noise level scrambled my brain and traumatised me.'

154.   *The Plaintiff vacated his dormitory room, Number 220, Holmes Hall, Harvard University, after the first session of abuse with the sonic device on March 1, 1987....*

155.   *....*

        'On April 2, two days after I had returned to my room, after a stay away of a month, the noise recurred at about mid-day and persisted for over an hour. It induced nausea and vertigo, and also caused pains in my heart.

        I immediately attended the law school clinic, and was seen by Dr. Stampfer, who noted that my critical faculties – blood pressure, pulse and temperature – had reached dangerous levels. She arranged for my admission to the Stillman Infirmary immediately.'

156.   *The Stillman Infirmary, referred to in the previous paragraph, is a private hospital operated by Harvard University, and is staffed by its employees. The Plaintiff's admis-*

sion there lasted about one week ....

157.   Shortly after his discharge from the Stillman Infirmary,
        and his return to his dormitory accommodation at Room
        220, Holmes Hall, the Plaintiff was subjected to a third
        bout of the sonic abuse.

> "The third distinct occasion when the noise occurred
> was on April 12, at about mid-day. On this occasion
> the noise persisted for about fifteen minutes and was
> extremely loud. It caused a severe pain in both my ears,
> and this pain still persists. As a result of this pain I was
> given medication by a Dr. Drake of the Stillman Infir-
> mary, and was also treated by Dr. Kiskaden, an ear spe-
> cialist at the Infirmary. He diagnosed a problem with
> my hearing and in particular with my right ear."

158.   The Plaintiff's refusal to succumb to the cowardly and
        appalling abuse that was taking place did not result in a
        cessation of same. This reflects the fact that the orders to
        conduct the campaign of abuse were coming from the top,
        were bitter and implacable. Neither the operatives of the
        sonic device, nor any Harvard personnel who might be
        expected to interfere, were in a position to do so.

> 'The noise re-occurred on April 25, and persisted for
> about three hours. Two other residents of Holmes Hall
> heard the noise, namely Bill Markham and Bob Wilkins.
> This was the first occasion in which I had corrobora-
> tion of the noise in the room, and I immediately tele-
> phoned Harvard Police, who sent a security officer to
> investigate the complaint. Apart from myself, the other
> two residents of the hall were available to give state-
> ments, but the security officer said that he did not have
> authority to take statements.'

159.   The latter averment is one of numerous indications that
        the ongoing abuse was authorised by Harvard administ-
        trators – lower level administrators, including the uni-
        versity police, did not see themselves as being in a posi-
        tion to interfere.

111

By 1992, when the complaint against Harvard was being drafted, five years experience had been gained in the Irish legal system concerning the universities' litigation strategy and tactics. This experience was reflected in the complaint filed in 1992.

80. *Furthermore, it can be assumed that Harvard University will contemplate an approach to the case in much the same manner as University College Cork approached the related pension case in the Irish courts. That may be summarised in four strategies. Firstly, it would seek to prevent any hearing of the case. Secondly, it would seek to manipulate any hearing that is necessitated. Thirdly, it would seek to discredit the Plaintiff at any hearing.*

81. *Fourthly, and most importantly, no relevant witnesses or documents would be presented or adduced in court on the part of Harvard University. "*

The foregoing predictions in the complaint in 1992 as to Harvard's approach to the litigation in the federal court system were prophetic. Throughout – at the levels of the District Court, Court of Appeals and the Supreme Court – what is consistently obvious is the aberrational dealing with the case within the federal judicial system. This dealing raised the inference of behind-the-scenes manipulations that were designed to kill the case in a summary manner and without publicity.

22 Harvard's Admission of Sonic Abuse

Harvard had avoided the personal injuries case in the Irish courts simply by refusing to acknowledge the jurisdiction. It ignored a formal request in 1991 to accede to that jurisdiction. Subsequently, in the Irish courts, Harvard failed to provide representation in both the High and Supreme courts when cited in the motion to serve notice of the Summons outside the jurisdiction. Harvard did not have that option in the courts of the United States. When served with the complaint that was filed on December 30, 1992, its initial response was to feign complete ignorance:-

"   HARVARD UNIVERSITY
      CAMBRIDGE • MASSACHUSETTS • 02138

Allan A. Ryan, Jr.   Holyoke Center 980
University Attorney   1350 Massachusetts Avenue
                                Cambridge, Massachusetts 02138
                                (067) 495-0525 Fax 495-5079
                                            January 13, 1993

*   Re: Denis Martin Linehan v. Harvard University*
Dear Mr. Linehan:
Harvard University received your complaint as filed in the United States District Court. In order that I might respond appropriately, please tell me what affiliation you had with Harvard. If you were a student, please let me know the program in which you were enrolled and the dates of your attendance.

*   This information is not clear from your complaint, and I write directly to you rather than file a motion to dismiss. Once I have the information, I will file an answer or otherwise be in touch with you.*   *Sincerely,*
*   Allan A. Ryan, Jr. "*

Thirteen days after the foregoing letter, on January 26, 1994, Harvard altered its defence posture. In the formal answer to the complaint served on that day, Harvard admitted my affiliation in the case, but denied the sonic and other abuse.

"   *The United States District Court*
*   District of Massachusetts*
Denis Martin Linehan,   )
*   Plaintiff,*   ) *Civil Action No. 92-13089*
MA
*   v.*   )
Harvard University,   ) *Answer of Defendant*
*   Defendant*   ) *Harvard University*
)

113

2-314.   Defendant admits that plaintiff was a graduate stu-
dent at Harvard Law School in the academic year 1986-87.
Defendant denies that it implanted a sonic device in plaintiff's
dormitory room in order to terminate plaintiff from the gradu-
ate program (¶¶ 101, 153-55, et seq.) or for any other reason.
Defendant denies that it abused plaintiff or otherwise acted
wrongfully or tortiously...."

Even prior to the petition to the American Supreme Court,
a vital turning point was reached in September, 1993. At
that time, Harvard **admitted** the sonic abuse in 1987.

   After more than six years of intensive litigation, Harvard made that critical admission of the sonic abuse in its
motion to dismiss the complaint in the federal District
Court on limitation grounds that was served on September 28, 1993. In order to rely on the defence that the limitations period had expired prior to the filing of the complaint, Harvard was constrained to rely on my knowledge
of the sonic abuse between March and May, 1987.

> *Defendant Harvard University's*
> *Motion to Dismiss the Complaint*

the complaint asserts two grounds on which the statute of limi-
tations is tolled. Both grounds are without foundation. First,
plaintiff asserts that in 1989 Harvard University engaged in
fraud to conceal the existence of the cause of action. Compl. ¶ ¶
187, 188. However, the plaintiff elsewhere asserts that he
knew of Harvard's installation of the sonic device, and the
injuries it had caused him, in May 1987 when he was admit-
ted to hospital. Compl. ¶ 305. This admission negates any
claim of a fraudulent concealment of the cause of action sufficient
to toll the statute of limitations....

   The admission of the sonic abuse in Harvard's motion
to dismiss was subsequently repeated in Harvard's brief for
the appellee filed in the federal Court of Appeals that was
served on February 3, 1994. This maintained the "u-turn"

by Harvard that had been adopted in its motion to dismiss.
"   *Brief for Appellee*

....

Plaintiff asserted in the complaint that he knew of Harvard's "sonic abuse," and the injuries it allegedly caused him, in May 1987, when he was admitted to a hospital. Complaint, ¶¶ 304, 305. The District Court implicitly found this admission sufficient to negate plaintiff's claim (Complaint, ¶¶ 187, 188) that Harvard had fraudulently concealed its alleged acts and had thus tolled the statute of limitations....

Plaintiff now argues (Br. 24) that the statute did not begin to run in 1987 because he did not then know which "Harvard University administrators" allegedly placed the sonic device, nor was he then "familiar with the nature of sonic devices and their usage for offensive purposes." These assertions are irrelevant. The general rule in personal injury actions is that the cause of action accrues when the plaintiff is injured." Riley v. Presnell. supra, 409 Mass. at 243. In cases subject to the "discovery rule," the cause of action accrues when the plaintiff "knew or had reason to know that he had been harmed by the defendant's conduct." ....

It may seem ironic – even to Harvard – that after six years of evading the issue of sonic abuse, and liability therefor, it would eventually admit it and indeed report that admission in formal pleadings in both a U.S. District Court and a U.S. Court of Appeals.

The catalytic reason for the admissions was legal, linked of course to the related one of financial liability. In liaison with U.C.C., Harvard had prolonged the pension litigation in Ireland in 1987 and thereafter in every conceivable way in order to create an efflux of time such as would give rise to a limitations defence. The general rule in personal injuries cases is that a case must be commenced within three years after its accrual.

When finally faced with the personal injuries case,

eventually Harvard plumbed for the limitations defence that it had worked at so assiduously with U.C.C. after 1987. However, in order to rely on that defence, it had to plead the victim's knowledge of the abuse and injuries at the time they occurred. Otherwise, it could not argue that the three years limitation period had elapsed before the complaint was filed in December, 1992.

Ultimately, therefore, Harvard law school may be said to have fallen foul of its own chicanery – having created an artificial defence, it had to admit the truth in order to rely on that defence. Harvard had been *hoist with its own petard.*

Apart from Harvard's formal admissions of the sonic abuse in the federal District and Appeals Courts, other proofs of the retaliatory abuse and injuries inflicted at Harvard between March and May, 1987, were also put on the record in the American federal court system. For instance, two letters dated May 19 and 20, 1987, from Frederick Snyder, Harvard administrator, clearly prove the breaches of contracts that had occurred at that time.

Following my confinement in intensive care at The Malden Hospital, Massachusetts, on May 10, 1987, independent medical evidence existed as to the cause and nature of the injuries sustained at Harvard. Shortly thereafter, and several weeks before the conferring of degrees on June 11, 1987, Harvard broke its contracts to provide accommodation and medical and other services in order to distance itself from liability. Through Snyder I was requested to leave Harvard.

"

HARVARD LAW SCHOOL
CAMBRIDGE •
MASSACHUSETTS• 02138

Assistant Dean for
International and Comparative Legal Studies
and Administrator of the
Graduate Program

116

Mr. Denis Linehan   *May 19, 1987*
Harvard Law School
Cambridge MA 02138
Dear Denis:

   This is to assure you that with the submission of a satisfactory paper to professor Kraakman, you will have met the formal requirements for the award of the LL.M. degree this June, 1987. I hope you have a pleasant return journey to Ireland in the next several days, and wish you all the best there.

                    Sincerely,
                    Frederick E. Snyder "

Snyder's letter of May 19, 1987, was followed by another in similar terms of the following day – the thrust of the correspondence was that I should return to Ireland *in the next several days.*

23 Denials of Oral Hearings

No proper or fair hearing, or adequate opportunity to present the personal injuries case, was afforded in either the American federal district or appeal courts.Thus, no hearing of any kind took place in the U.S. District Court. That is proved by the following extract from Harvard's reply brief that was served on February 3, 1994:-

   "On November 15, 1993, Judge Mazzone .... allowed Harvard's motion to dismiss. Contrary to Petitioner's belief, there was no hearing; neither party requested one. See Local Rule 7.1(D);...."

Harvard's assertion that neither party had requested a hearing was clearly false, as it proved from the complaint in the case dated December 30, 1992, as follows:-

   "   *Jury Prayer*
   The Plaintiff asserts any right he may have to Trial by Jury.
   Respectfully Submitted
   Plaintiff   "

On November 15, 1993, Judge Mazzone, of the federal District Court in Boston for the District of Massachusetts, without any hearing and without providing an adequate opportunity to be heard otherwise, granted Harvard's motion to dismiss on limitations grounds in the following peremptory manner; *"Allowed. The Plaintiff has not opposed the motion, and clearly, the plaintiff's claims are time-barred."*

This virtually surreptitious dealing with the case was followed on the following day by an order in the following terms:

"UNITED STATES DISTRICT COURT
DISTRICT OF MASSACHUSETTS

Denis Martin Linehan
    (Plaintiff)   *CIVIL ACTION*
        vs.   *No.   92 - 13089 - MA*
Harvard University
    (Defendant)

ORDER OF DISMISSAL

Mazzone   D.J.
In accordance with the court's allowance of the defendant's motion to dismiss on Nov. 15, 1993, it is hereby ORDERED that the above-entitled action be and hereby is dismissed.

By the Court,

Nov. 16, 1993   *Deputy Clerk*
    Date
(5/89)   "

One does not need to be a lawyer to appreciate the peculiar manner in which the District Court dealt with the case. Apart from the denial of a hearing, no analysis of either facts or law was offered in a case where $10 million were claimed.

An oral hearing was also denied by the U.S. Court of Appeals. That is proved by the following notice from the court clerk dated February 24, 1994:-

"To Counsel:
In accordance with Rule 34 of the Federal Rules of Appel-

late Procedure, as amended effective December 1, 1993, this is to advise you that the three judges of a panel, after examination of the briefs and record, are unanimously of the opinion that oral argument is not needed in this case.

Consequently, under F.R.A.P. Rule 34(a), this case will be taken on submission of briefs without oral argument."

Moreover, no opportunity was given by the Court of Appeals, to reply to certain written submissions made by Harvard. That is proved by the following letter dated June 10, 1994, from the court clerk:-

"Dear Mr. Linehan:

I acknowledge receipt of your letter dated May 31, 1994 requesting to file a supplemental reply brief. Your letter of May 31, 1994 and this Court's judgment of June 9, 1994 crossed in the mail. The Court having entered its judgment in this case has made its decision. Your next recourse, if you so wish to take it, is to file, within 14 days from the judgment, a petition for rehearing with a suggestion for rehearing en banc.

Very truly yours,

Francis P. Scigliano, Clerk "

Thus, even the hearing based on written submissions afforded by the first circuit was severely restricted.

In sum, I was not afforded the usual facilities to make out my case either at first instance or on appeal. The court record prior to the petition to the American Supreme Court was therefore unusually sparse.

The judgment and order of the federal Court of Appeals merits substantial reproduction on one ground, in particular, namely, it embodies the Harvard admission of the sonic abuse and its resort to a limitations defence in order to avoid liability for the resulting injuries. The judgment and order, that were entered on June 9, 1994, are in part as follows:

"[NOT FOR PUBLICATION]
UNITED STATES COURT OF APPEALS
FOR THE FIRST CIRCUIT

APPEAL FROM THE UNITED STATES DISTRICT
COURT
FOR THE DISTRICT OF MASSACHUSETTS
[Hon. A. David Mazzone, U.S. District Judge]
Before
Torruella, Cyr and Stahl,
Circuit Judges

*Per Curiam. Plaintiff appeals the district court's dismissal
of his diversity suit as time-barred under Massachusetts
three-year statute of limitations for personal injury actions.
The complaint alleges that between March and May, 1987,
while plaintiff was enrolled in a graduate studies program
at Harvard Law School, defendant subjected him to sonic
abuse from a remote controlled device installed in close prox-
imity to his dormitory room. Plaintiff claims that defendant's
wrongful actions were motivated by a vendetta that had its
origin in an employment dispute between the plaintiff and
University College Cork in Ireland.*

Having identified the sonic abuse within the Harvard
law school complex as the basis of the claim for compensation, the opinion of the Court of Appeals turned to the
issue of limitation. Harvard had formally pleaded that,
because I knew of the sonic abuse in 1987, the general rule
of a three year limitations period applied.

*The complaint was filed on December 10, 1992, more than
five years after the dates of alleged injury. Plaintiff argues,
however, that the three-year statute of limitations is tolled
by (1) fraudulent concealment.*

*(1) A defendant's alleged fraud may toll the limitations
period only if it "conceals the cause of .... action from the
knowledge of the person entitled to bring it ...." Mass. Gen.
L. ch. 260, § 12.* **Plaintiff's complaint asserts, however,
that he was aware of the alleged sonic abuse and his
physical injury at the time it occurred. His theory that
Harvard is responsible for the alleged tort is built**

almost entirely on actions and statements by Harvard personnel of which he was aware in 1986 and 1987. In addition, as early as May, 1987, plaintiff sought legal assistance to litigate or mediate this claim against Harvard. "[A] cause of action is not concealed from one who has knowledge of the facts that create it ...."

The case against Harvard also included claims for breaches of contracts. The limitation period for such is six years, and therefore it could hardly be argued that the complaint had been filed outside the six year period. The Court of Appeals overcome that difficulty by treating these contracts as *incidental.*

(4) The gravamen of plaintiff's complaint is that defendant engaged in physically injurious acts against him. Although he alleges incidental contracts that impose other obligations, the personal injury he claims does not arise from those contracts. Accordingly, the three-year statute of limitations governs this action.

The case against Harvard had been proved in the Irish courts, and had resulted in a judgment of the Irish Supreme Court in the pension case against U.C.C. on July 9, 1992. Under general legal principles, found in both national and international law, courts acknowledge the findings of other courts. These principles were readily side-stepped by the Court of Appeals.

(5) The purported judgment of the Irish Supreme Court awarding to plaintiff a pension from University College Cork is irrelevant to the issues before us. Harvard was not a party to the alleged Irish litigation. The Irish court's alleged refusal to issue a summons for service on Harvard because of "forum conveniens," does not, as plaintiff urges, evidence a determination by that court of the Massachusetts limitations question.

Accordingly, the judgment below is affirmed. "

Once a policy decision to find for one litigant has been made, it is relatively easy for any court to justify its findings by a selective approach to the evidence before it and to the legal interpretation that is put on that evidence. To a lay person, the end product of the opinion can be made to appear reasoned, comprehensive and plausible. On an initial reading, the First Circuit's opinion gave such an impression.

However, the opinion had erred fundamentally in certain respects. In particular, without any reference to relevant facts and law, it assumed that the personal injuries cause of action had accrued against Harvard upon my admission to intensive care at The Malden Hospital, Massachusetts, in May, 1987. In consequence, it implicitly made the incorrect deduction that the personal injuries cause of action had become time barred on or about May, 1990, such that the complaint filed in December, 1992, was out of time.

24 The Path to the American Supreme Court

At nine, the number of reasons advanced to the Supreme Court for granting certiorari was unusually high. Five of these related to the disposition of the case in the lower courts. It was maintained and proved that an oral hearing had been denied in both the District Court and the Court of Appeals. Moreover, neither court had given an adequate opportunity to present the case even in writing. Two of these reasons derived from the proceedings of related and parallel cases in Ireland, the records and judgments in which were contended to be of relevance in different senses to the case. Both the District Court and the Court of Appeals had refused to acknowledge five years of proceedings in the Irish courts between 1987 and 1992, including a decision of the Irish Supreme Court. It was maintained that this breached international law and estoppel principles. The remaining two reasons referred to fundamental errors that were alleged in the approach to substantive issues by the First Circuit. It was maintained that the personal injuries case had not accrued until 1992 or 1993, and therefore Harvard's limitation defence should fail. It was also maintained that Harvard's breaches of contracts were governed by a six years' limitations period.

The Supreme Court comprises nine justices. These include the Chief Justice and eight associate justices. In the 1993-1994 Term, the court was made up of the following members:- *Chief Justice W. H. Rehnquist, and Associate Justices H. A. Blackmun, J. P. Stevens, S. Day O'Connor, A. Scalia, A. M. Kennedy, D. H. Souter, C. Thomas and R. B. Ginsburg.*

Harvard, through its *alumni*, is represented throughout the different spheres of American government, including the judiciary. Nevertheless, I was surprised to discover the extent of the direct connection of Harvard with the Supreme Court in terms of its membership. That connection was referred to in a cover story of Time magazine in 1986 entitled *Happy Birthday Fair Harvard.* The article, that marked the three hundred and fiftieth anniversary of Harvard, recited the connection as follows:-

"A reception last winter in Washington honoured 40 high-ranking presidential appointees with the Harvard connection. Among them: Federal Reserve Chairman Paul Voricker and five Cabinet members.

Absent from the party were Chief Justice Nominee William Rehnquist (M.A., '50) and three of the Supreme Court's Associate Justices, all veterans of the Harvard Law School, where Oliver Wendell Holmes Jr., and Felix Frankfurter learned their torts, and where a pragmatic innovation called the case-study system changed legal education in America. Says Alumnus Richard Darman, Deputy Secretary of the Treasury: 'I cannot imagine the influence has ever been higher than it is now'."

In 1986, of the nine members of the Supreme Court, four were graduates of Harvard law school. That number had risen to five by 1994, after president Bill Clinton had appointed associate justice Ginsburg.

A motion to extend the time for filing the petition was filed on July 22, 1994, pursuant to rule 13.2. This application was to extend the normal filing period of ninety days by another sixty days. That application was granted by associate justice D.H. Souter. This extended the time for filing the petition up to and including November 6, 1994. It was the first and only helpful ruling given in the prosecution of the case in the American legal system. The court correspondence is as follows:

"   SUPREME COURT OF THE UNITED STATES
                    OFFICE OF THE CLERK
                 WASHINGTON, DC 20543

WILLIAM K. SUTER   AREA CODE 202
Clerk of the Court   479-3011

Mr. Denis M. Linehan   *July 28, 1994*

22, Summerstown Grove, Wilton,

Cork, Ireland.

Re: Denis Martin Linehan, v. Harvard University
*   Application No. A-59*

Dear Mr. Linehan,

The application for an extension of time within which to file a petition for a writ of certiorari in the above-entitled case has been presented to Justice Souter, who on July 28, 1994, signed an order extending the time to and including November 6, 1994.

A copy of the Justice's Order is enclosed.

                         Sincerely,
                         William K. Suter, Clerk
                         By Clayton R. Higgins, Jr.,
                         Assistant Clerk

Note: For Your Information: A copy of this letter has been sent to all interested parties shown on the attached notification list. "

The foregoing correspondence enclosed the following Order of the Supreme Court.:–

"   *ORDER*
Upon Consideration of the application of counsel for the

petitioner,
IT IS ORDERED that the time for filing a petition for a writ of
certiorari in the above-entitled case, be and the same is hereby,
extended to and including November 6 , 1994.

/s/ David H. Souter
Associate Justice of the Supreme
Court of the United States

Dated this <u>28th</u>
day of July, 1994 "

A motion to exceed page limits in the petition was filed on October 7, 1994, pursuant to rule 33. That application was necessitated by reason of the standard limitation of petitions to 65 pages, exclusive of contents and appendices. That limitation is highly restrictive, but was particularly so in this case where an oral hearing had been denied in both lower courts.

The application to exceed page limits was denied by order of Associate Justice Souter dated October 13, 1994, but notice of this denial was received only on October 27, 1994. That allowed less than 6 weekdays to adapt and produce the petition that ran to a total of 425 pages.

Nevertheless, that was done on time by a notice that formally deleted the excess pages, and the petition was timely filed by certified first class post on November 5, 1994.

The petition was a comprehensive document. I, and several research assistants and colleagues, had worked intensively on it for nearly a five month period between June and November, 1994.

In addition, the petition referred to the written submission to the Irish Supreme Court made in July, 1992, and same was furnished to the American Supreme Court as an exhibit. The latter document totals about 1,234 pages in length.

In other words, in the context of the petition, a total of nearly 1,700 pages of evidence and argument was furnished to the American Supreme Court.

The petition, and the evidence furnished with it,

clearly proved the abuse and injuries at Harvard in 1987. It also proved Harvard's admission of same in its effort to rely on a statute of limitations defence. The petition also proved the denial of any meaningful hearing of the case in either the District Court or the Court of Appeals.

25 Denial of Filing

Great care and considerable resources had been expended between July and November, 1994, to ensure the adequacy of the filing in the Supreme Court. When filed on November 5, 1994, no reasonable doubt could have existed on that score. Nevertheless, the filing on that date marked the onset of more than two months of sharp conflict in relation to the filing. On behalf of the Supreme Court, this conflict was conducted through the Office of the Clerk.

The clerk's office first returned the papers with letter dated November 21, 1994, and I in turn returned the papers with letter dated December 3, 1994. The same cycle was repeated almost immediately with letter from the clerk's office dated December 9, 1994, and return letter from me dated December 23, 1994.

These exchanges were marked by direct conflict on matters of readily apparent facts. On receiving the papers for the second time, the clerk's office immediately returned them to me on the basis of an alleged absence from the petition of the rulings by the U.S. District Court and the Court of Appeals.

The reasons for the return of the papers on this occasion were as spurious as on the first occasion. The clerk's office, under the manipulation of parties behind the scenes, was engaging in pure fiction in an effort to deny the petition that had been filed as well as the evidence contained in it.

With covering letter dated December 23, 1994, I again returned the papers to the clerk's office. That letter challenged the authority of the clerk's office to raise further new objections after initial objections had been met. It also challenged the latest objections, and raised the issue of referring the dispute either to the Supreme Court or to an individual Justice other than a Harvard *alumnus*.

26   The Buck Stops . . . There

By early December, 1994, it had become obvious that the $10 million personal injuries case against Harvard was being stonewalled in the clerk's office of the Supreme Court.

Commencing with correspondence dated December 23, 1994, two types of representations were made to parties external to the Office of the Clerk of the Supreme Court. First, I circularised copies of my correspondence to that office to selected notice parties. These included:- the Irish prime minister, John Bruton; deputy prime minister, Dick Spring and a number of Irish ministers including Nora Owen, Niamh Bhreathnach, Ruairi Quinn, Proinsias De Rossa and Pat Rabbitte. They also included:- the Irish president, Mary Robinson; the Irish ambassador to the United States, Dermot Gallagher and the Irish attorney general, Dermot Gleeson. Also circularised, from the standpoint of the United States, were:- Jean Kennedy-Smith, American ambassador to Ireland, and Mr. Edward Kennedy, United States senator.

The second type of representation consisted of a standardised letter. This outlined the history of the scandal and sought interventions. The letter to Dermot Gleeson, who had recently been appointed attorney general, is a facsimile of those sent to the other notice parties:-

Dear Mr. Gleeson,   *December 23, 1994*
Re: Myself v Harvard University
Processing of Case by United States Supreme Court
Injury at Harvard in 1987

I was seriously injured at Harvard University in 1987 while in employment with University College Cork. That has greatly affected my capacity to earn a livelihood in the meantime. Both universities have refused to pay compensation, although the injuries and the responsibility have been proved and admitted in both the Irish and American legal systems.

Proceedings in American Courts

...

I was denied a hearing in the U.S. District Court in Boston. I was also denied an oral hearing in the Court of Appeals, First Circuit. After extensive proofs of the injuries and the admissions of responsibility were timely and properly filed in the U.S. Supreme Court on November 5 last, the Clerk's Office in that court has twice returned the paper for patently bogus reasons.

...

I believe that this matter is clearly of relevance to the relations between both states, and the reciprocal treatment of citizens and their interests in each. I also believe that the matter is of relevance to you by reason of your good offices.

Accordingly, I now enclose also a copy certified letter dated December 23, 1994, to the Clerk's Office, United States Supreme Court, with which I have returned for the second time the papers timely and correctly filed on November 5, 1994. I trust that you may work to ensure that the case is dealt with properly and efficiently by the Supreme Court.

Issue of Compensation

It is obviously scandalous that no compensation has been paid, notwithstanding the proofs and admissions that are now on record in two legal systems. ...

If further information is required, I shall be glad to provide same. I can be reached by correspondence at the above address or through accommodation telephone number (021) 310876 or fax (021) 310983.

I thank you in anticipation of your good offices, and I look forward to hearing from you.

Yours sincerely,
Encl.   *Denis M. Linehan*

Of the twelve notice parties from whom intervention was sought, eleven replied shortly thereafter. The only exception was Dermot Gleeson, Irish attorney general. Mr. Gleeson had acted as senior counsel for U.C.C. in the 1986 High Court case. Moreover, his eventual reply to the correspondence, made on May 15, 1995, occurred only days before the Irish police become implicated in the scandal.

Of the eleven notice parties who did reply in the normal course to the request for representation, all refused to intervene. A wide variety of reasons were given, some of which were obviously valid and some of which were obviously not. All refusals, except that of senator Edward Kennedy, came in the period between January 10 and 19, 1995.

The Irish president, Mary Robinson, who is herself a graduate of Harvard law school, replied by letter dated January 10, 1995, as follows:-

"

OIFIG RÚNA' AN UACHTARÁIN
BAILE ATHA CLIATH 8.
OFFICE OF THE SECRETARY TO THE PRESIDENT
DUBLIN 8

10 January, 1995.
Mr. Denis M. Linehan
Legal Advice & Consultancy Services
22 Summerstown Grove
Wilton
Cork
Dear Mr. Linehan,
The President, Mary Robinson, has asked me to thank you for your letter of 23rd December, 1994.

The President was very sorry to learn of the circumstances described in your letter but regrets that, due to the constitutional con-

straints of her Office, it would not be appropriate for her to intervene.

She hopes you will understand and sends her good wishes.

Yours sincerely,

Kay Gleeson

Assistant Secretary to the President

TEILEAFON: +353-1-677 2815 FACS: +353-1-671 0529 "

It is noteworthy that on June 12, 1997, President Robinson was given the post of United Nations Human Rights Commissioner, the position to be taken up later in the year.

The Irish ambassador to the United States, Dermot Gallagher, notified his refusal to intervene in the following letter dated January 12, 1995:-

" AMBASÁID NA hEIREANN   EMBASSY OF IRELAND

TELEPHONE: (202) 462-3939   2234 MASSACHUSETTS AVE.,N.W.

FAX: (202) 232-5993   WASHINGTON, D.C. 20008

12 January, 1995

Mr Denis M Linehan

22 Summerstown Grove

Wilton

Cork

IRELAND

Dear Mr Linehan

I have received your letter of 23 December 1994.

I note that you have written to the Clerk of the US Supreme Court and that you have queried the basis on which certain papers were returned to you by his Office in early December.

I am afraid that this Embassy cannot evaluate the specific legal points which you have raised with the Clerk's Office regarding the return of these papers. In the circumstances, I would suggest that you seek advice on the matter from a legal firm in the United States which is familiar with the practices and procedures of the Supreme Court of this country.

Yours sincerely

Dermot Gallagher

Ambassador   "

Senator Kennedy is also a graduate of Harvard law

school. In addition, he had been a member of the Committee on the Judiciary in the much publicised Clarence Thomas-Anita Hill hearings of October 11-13, 1991.

These hearings had taken place after Clarence Thomas, a Circuit Court judge, had been nominated to the Supreme Court. At that point, allegations of sexual harassment against him almost ten years previously were made by Anita Hill, then a law professor at the university of Oklahoma. Judge Thomas categorically denied these, and attributed them to an orchestrated campaign to sabotage his nomination. In the course of the hearings, he remarked that:-

".... If it can happen to me it can happen to anybody, any time over any issue. Our institutions are being controlled by people who will stop at nothing. They went around this country looking for dirt, not information on Clarence Thomas, dirt. Anybody with any dirt, anything, late at night calls, calls at work, calls at home, badgering, anything, give us some dirt. I think that if our country has reached this point we are in trouble ...."

In the event, the senate confirmed Clarence Thomas's nomination as a Supreme Court justice on November 15, 1991, by a majority of four, with 52 for confirmation and 48 against.

Senator Kennedy responded to my correspondence of December 23, 1994 by letter dated March 13, 1995:-

"EDWARD M. KENNEDY
MASSACHUSETTS

United States Senate
WASHINGTON, DC 20510-2101

March 13, 1995

Mr. Denis M. Linehan, Esq.
22 Summerstown Grove, Wilton
Cork, Ireland
Dear Mr. Linehan:
The enclosed documents were sent to Senator Kennedy's office without a cover letter.

They are returned to you because under the Privacy Act of 1974 it is required that you write a letter to the Senator requesting his assistance before a federal agency can release any information about your case.

When you return these documents with your letter to Senator Kennedy, a letter of support is usually written on your behalf. In this case, however, that would not be possible. As a U.S. Senator on the Judiciary Committee, it would be inappropriate for him to intervene in matters before the courts or those pertaining to a state's judicial process.

I hope this information will be of assistance to you. The Senator extends his best wishes.

With best wishes.

Sincerely,
Barbara Souliotis
State Administrative Assistant

2400 JFK Federal Building
Boston, MA 02203

PRINTED ON RECYCLED PAPER "

Although his membership of the judiciary committee precluded him from direct intervention, nevertheless, senator Kennedy's reply adverted to a statutory procedure whereby government information on the case could be obtained.

The foregoing litany of refusals was significant because it left me back at square one in dealing with the clerk's office of the Supreme Court. It is also significant because none of the parties mentioned can take credit for the outcome of the dispute with the clerk's office.

27 Early Wins

In view of the initial and intermediate positions taken by the clerk's office of the Supreme Court, the preliminary victories in the case in January, 1995, are all the more remarkable. One of these victories was against Harvard, and was implicit. The second was against the clerk's office and was explicit.

It had become clear during the proceedings in the lower courts that Harvard was legally pinning its defence hopes on a limitations defence. Harvard's position was simple – completely immoral – but simple, and can be summarised thus:

"We acknowledge the sonic abuse and the injuries it caused but the Plaintiff was too late in filing his Complaint in order to legally recover compensation."

Having made that defence, and succeeded with it, in both the federal District Court in Boston and the Court of Appeals, there was no obvious reason why it should not have repeated this defence in the Supreme Court. Whatever the reasons for its failure to plead, Harvard's omission so to do was an important victory – the university did not have the proverbial two words to say for itself in the Supreme Court.

The correspondence from the clerk's office during the first half of January, 1995, prove a deepening entrenchment on its part. The reasons given for refusing to acknowledge that the petition had been filed on November 5, 1994, multiplied and became more obviously fictitious at this time. By letter dated January 5, 1995, no less than seven reasons were given for refusing to acknowledge the filings – all reasons were clearly false. That letter reads as follows:-

" SUPREME COURT OF THE UNITED STATES
OFFICE OF THE CLERK
WASHINGTON, DC 20543-0001

WILLIAM K. SUTER   AREA CODE 202
CLERK OF THE COURT   479-3011

January 5, 1995

Re: Linehan v. Harvard University
Petitioner: Denis M. Linehan
The above-entitled petition for writ of certiorari was originally post-

marked November 5, 1994 and received again on January 4, 1995.
The papers are returned for the following reason(s):

> *No motion for leave to proceed in forma pauperis, signed by*
> *the petitioner or by counsel, is attached. Rules 34.2 and 39.*
> *The motion must be signed.*
> *The petition fails to comply with the content requirements*
> *of Rule 14, in that the petition does not contain:*
> *The questions presented for review. Rule 14.1(1).*
> *A reference to the opinions below. Rule 14.1(d).*
> *A concise statement of the grounds on which jurisdiction is*
> *invoked.   Rule 14.1(e).*
> *The reasons relied on for the allowance of the writ.   Rules*
> *10 and 14.1(j).*

The appendix to the petition does not contain the following docu-
ments required by Rule 14.1(k):

> *The lower court opinion(s) must be appended.*

It is impossible to determine the timeliness of the petition without
the lower court opinions.

By letter dated January 11, 1995, the entrenched negative
position of the clerk's office in refusing to acknowledge the
filing was maintained. The reasons given differed again from
those given on January 5, 1995; however, they were as equally
groundless. At this stage, the objections by the clerk's office
had grown increasingly wild. Thus, in the letter dated January
11, 1995, from the clerk's office, reliance was placed on the
non-filing of an affidavit in support of the *in forma pauperis*
motion. This was flatly contradicted in a reply dated January
20, 1995.

It transpired that what may be termed the *battle for the*
filing of the petition had been won even prior to the dis-
patch of the letter dated January 20, 1995. On January 24,
1995, a remarkable letter was received from the clerk's
office that showed that this battle had been won on January 18, 1995. That letter is in the following terms:
" SUPREME COURT OF THE UNITED STATES
OFFICE OF THE CLERK
WASHINGTON, DC 20543-0001

AREA CODE 202
479-3011

January 18, 1995

....

Re: Denis Martin Linehan,
*   v. Harvard University*
*   No. 94-7657*

Dear Mr. Linehan:

The petition for a writ of certiorari in the above entitled case was docketed in this Court on November 5, 1994 as No. 94-7657.

A form is enclosed for notifying opposing counsel that the case was docketed.

> *Very truly yours,*
> *William K. Suter, Clerk*
> *by*
> *Francis J. Lorson*

Enclosures   *Chief Deputy Clerk "*

The above letter marked a major victory in the litigation. It proved that the entire course of conduct by the Office of the Clerk of the Supreme Court in refusing to acknowledge the filing of the petition between November 21, 1994, and January 18, 1995, had been spurious. Further dealings with the case would bear the stamp of the Supreme Court of the United States – the matter was no longer formally being dealt with by clerks.

28 Issues Before the American Supreme Court

An appeal involves a rehearing of a case on the merits. In contrast, certiorari is a discretionary remedy whereby a court may supervise a lower court or tribunal. This supervision is typically exercised by quashing the decision of the lower court or tribunal, and ordering that it reconsider the dispute in accordance with directions given.

Since 1988, it is no longer possible to appeal directly on the merits from an appellate court to the Supreme Court.

Instead, one can apply to that court only for the supervisory and discretionary writ of certiorari. The discretionary remedy of certiorari may be granted if a lower court has exceeded its jurisdiction, or has acted unfairly by denying natural justice or has erred in law. The *discretionary* character of certiorari is emphasised in the Supreme Court rules. Moreover, these rules introduce another prerequisite for the granting of certiorari that is not common in the general law, namely, there must be *special and important reasons* for granting the remedy.

One of the grounds upon which certiorari may be granted is where the lower courts have acted unfairly by denying natural justice. Five of the nine reasons submitted to the Supreme Court for granting the remedy in this case turned on this ground.

The arguments for certiorari in this respect seemed watertight. Thus, neither the District Court nor the Court of Appeals had granted an oral hearing. Moreover, the Court of Appeals had even restricted the written evidence before it. That is illustrated by an episode that occurred between May 20 and June 10, 1994. On May 20, 1994, Harvard served by post a supplemental memorandum that reads in relevant part as follows:-

"A document in Mr. Linehan's reply demonstrates conclusively that his claim is barred by the statute of limitations. It is a letter from a solicitor in Ireland, representing Mr. Linehan, to an attorney in Providence, Rhode Island, discussing Mr. Linehan's allegations against Harvard University and a 'possible settlement of the claim.' Reply brief at 65.

The letter was written in June 1987. It provides extrinsic support to the acknowledgement in the complaint that Mr. Linehan was aware of the grounds for his claim at that time. In fact it demonstrates that Mr. Linehan was actively pursuing the matter with the assistance of counsel. This state of affairs plainly bars the present suit under Bowen v. Eli Lilly & Co., 408 Mass. 204 (1990). See Harvard University's brief at 3-4.

> *Respectfully submitted,*
> *PRESIDENT AND FELLOWS OF*
> *HARVARD COLLEGE "*

Because of the inaccurate and misleading nature of that memorandum, a request was made to the Court of Appeals by letter dated May 21, 1994, for leave to file a supplemental reply brief. Part of that letter reads as follows:-

Dear Sirs,

I am requesting leave to file a Supplemental Reply Brief herein in response to the Appellee's Supplemental Memorandum served on May 20 last.

At this juncture, I have three related points to make in this summary:-

1. The disinformation in said Supplemental Memorandum further illustrates my arguments that an oral hearing is necessary in this appeal. Accordingly, I am also repeating my request for same.

2. The arguments made in the second paragraph of the Supplemental Memorandum are unfounded either in fact or law. At this stage I make only one comment on same, i.e., Michael Keating, the Rhode Island counsel referred to in the Supplemental Memorandum, represented the Appellee's interests - not mine - in 1987 and thereafter. Mr. Keating in fact did me a great disservice.

Mr. Keating was introduced to me by David O'Connor of Massachusetts Mediation Service. I had been put in touch with David O'Connor in April 1987, through Frank Sander of Harvard Law School. ...

"An experienced mediator of Harvard disputes" was how Mr. Keating was referred to by David O'Connor. In sum, Mr. Keating was a "fixer" for Harvard. ...

That request was refused by letter dated June 10, 1994, on the basis it had *crossed in the mail* with the Court of Appeal's decision on June 9, 1994.

Dear Mr. Linehan:

I acknowledge receipt of your letter dated May 31, 1994 requesting to file a supplemental reply brief. Your letter of May

31, 1994 and this Court's judgment of June 9, 1994 crossed in the mail. The Court having entered its judgment in this case has made its decision. Your next recourse, if you so wish to take it, is to file, within 14 days from the judgment, a petition for rehearing with a suggestion for rehearing en banc.

Very truly yours

FPS/mam   *Francis P. Scigliano, Clerk "*

This was the second occasion on which the Court of Appeals had relied on a *crossing in the mail* for circumventing an application. In April, 1994, a request for an oral hearing was similarly discounted in this way.

In any event, the refusal to permit a supplemental reply brief in response to Harvard's supplemental memorandum served on May 20, 1994, meant that the Court of Appeals had made its decision on the basis of inaccurate and misleading information that no opportunity was given to correct.

The extraordinary manner in which both the U.S. District Court and the U.S. Court of Appeals had dealt with the case had given rise to a bizarre precedent – a case had reached the American Supreme Court without either party having appeared in any previous court!

In the petition to the Supreme Court, it was contended that the failure by the lower courts to provide either an oral hearing or an adequate opportunity to be heard breached the American constitution, natural justice as well as international law. One of the authorities relied on was the fifth amendment to the constitution, that is in relevant part as follows:-

".... nor shall any person .... be deprived of life, liberty, or property without due process of law."

Failure to provide a fair hearing is also generally recognised as constituting a breach of international law. Viewed objectively, in fact and in law, the arguments made for certiorari to the Supreme Court on the grounds of a denial of a hearing in the lower courts were unimpeachable.

One of the grounds upon which certiorari can be granted is where a lower court has erred in law. Two of the nine reasons submitted to the Supreme Court for granting certiorari in this case turned on this ground. These reasons, that were fully substantiated, referred to the manner in which the lower courts had sustained Harvard's limitations defence.

Harvard's limitation defence was at the heart of the petition that went to the Supreme Court. For that reason, it merits further examination.

The limitations defence was set out in the motion to dismiss the complaint served by Harvard on September 28, 1993, in the context of the proceedings in the U.S. District Court.

It is obvious from the motion to dismiss that Harvard's limitation defence contained two limbs. One referred to the personal injuries cause of action in the complaint, and the other referred to the contractual cause of action. These limbs merit separate examination, because of the centrality of the limitations defence to the issues that were before the Supreme Court.

The essence of Harvard's limitation defence in relation to the personal injuries claim was contained in three sentences of the motion to dismiss as follows:-

".... The statute of limitations in Massachusetts for personal injuries is three years ....

The complaint was filed on December 30, 1992 – more than five years after the alleged injury – and thus it is time-barred ....

the plaintiff elsewhere asserts that he knew of Harvard's installation of the sonic abuse, and the injuries it had caused him, in May, 1987 when he was admitted to a hospital ...."

The federal District Court had sustained that defence on November 15, 1993, without giving any reasons. The Court of Appeals had sustained it by an opinion entered on June 9, 1994. The Appeal Court's reasoning is important – in the Supreme Court petition, it was proven to be fundamentally flawed.

The Appeal Court's reasoning incorrectly assumed that the personal injuries cause of action had accrued, such as to start time running under the statute of limitations, at the time of the abuse and injuries at Harvard between March and May, 1987. Thus, the judgment reads in part as follows:-

"Plaintiff's complaint asserts, however, that he was aware of the alleged sonic abuse and his physical injury at the time it occurred. His theory that Harvard is responsible for the alleged tort is built almost entirely on actions and statements by Harvard personnel of which he was aware in 1986 and 1987."

In making the incorrect assumption that the personal injuries cause of action accrued in 1987, the Court of Appeals disregarded both material facts and relevant law, including its own precedents. Thus, in Massachusetts, as in most common law jurisdictions, a cause of action does not accrue until there is knowledge or reasonable notice of *all* elements of it.

Irrefutable proof was furnished in the Supreme Court petition that certain essential elements of the personal injuries cause of action remained unknown until the 1992-1993 period. These included, for instance, the nature, extent and permanency of the injuries caused in 1987 at Harvard. It was clear from the Doppler sonic tests that those injuries remained legally indeterminate until July 21, 1993. That was *after* the complaint in the case had been filed in 1992 - thus, until July 21, 1993, the personal injuries cause of action had not legally accrued.

Independent proof moreover was furnished to the Supreme Court that other lawyers had given their professional opinions that the personal injuries cause of action had not accrued against Harvard for limitations purposes in 1987 and 1988. These lawyers included the Rhode Island firm of Tillinghast, Collins & Graham, a firm selected from within Harvard in 1987 as potential mediators. As is stated and indicated in the following letter, that firm gave an opinion in 1988 that the personal injuries cause of action

against Harvard had not then accrued such as to start time
running under the statute of limitations.

" Edwin H. Hastings*
Alfred B. Stapleton
Eustace T. Pliakas
Robert McGarry*
DeWitte T. Kersh, Jr.
Peter J. McGinn*
Louise Durfee
John J. Partridg*
Stanley A. Bleecker
Joseph W. Walsh
Ernest C. Torres
David T. Riedel*
Robert W. Edwards, Jr.
Peter A. Sherman
James E. Purcell*
Normand G. Benoit*
Christopher H. Little*
Steven E. Snow
Stephen T. O'Neill
Stephen Lichatin III
James H. Hahn*
Constance A. Howes
Marilyn Shannon McConaghy*
John M. Bochnert
Richard H. Gregory III
Brian J. Spero*

Tillinghast, Collins & Graham
Counselors at Law

ONE OLD STONE SQUARE
PROVIDENCE, RHODE ISLAND 02903

(401) 456-1200

CABLE ADDRESS
T C G PVD
TELECOPIER
456-121

TELEX
952166

January 7, 1988

David M. Gilden
Daniel C. Waugh*
Fran R. Robins-Liben
Penelope W. Register
Erica Eisinger
Henry R. Kates
John H. Root*
John E. Bulman
William J. Clegg III
Kevin P. Gavin
William H. Jestings
Michael Kevorkian*
Daniel C. Bryant
Linda H. Carney
Gerald Parascandolo
Caroline M. Gilroy
Gretchen Sommerfeld
Roger E. Goodman
Craig S. Harwood

Counsel
J. Michael Keating, Jr.

Of Counsel
George C. Davis
Thomas R. Wickersham
William M. Sloane
R. Gordon Scott
Bayard Ewing
Edward J. Regan

*Member Massachusetts Bar

*Stephen J. Fortunato, Jr., Esq.
260 West Exchange Street
Providence, Rhode Island   02903
Re: Denis Linehan v. Harvard University
Dear Stephen
Thank you for reviewing the Linehan materials. Your conclu-
sions confirm our own. I will communicate your response to Mr.
Cuddigan....
    Thanks again for reviewing the Linehan materials. I know
you would have relished a solid case against the Crimson.*

                    Sincerely yours,
JMK/jta   *J. Michael Keating, Jr.*
cc: Joseph S. Cuddigan   "

In sum, in relation to the personal injuries claim, Harvard's limitation defence did not withstand scrutiny.

The complaint against Harvard also set out a breach of contract cause of action. Since the limitation period for same is six years, the filing of the complaint in 1992 was clearly timely.

Over $40,000 had been paid in respect of contracts pertaining to graduate studies, a fellowship, dormitory accommodation, university health services, linen services and other incidentals of obtaining a graduate degree from Harvard in 1987. The retaliatory abuse between March and May, 1987, had clearly involved a breach of certain of those contracts.

Harvard's limitations defence of the contract claim, as set out in its motion to dismiss the complaint, plumbed the depths of absurdity. It pleaded that:-

> ".... a plaintiff cannot extend the three-year statute of limitations by retooling claims for personal injury as claims for breach of a contract not to be injured."

This defence introduced the bizarre notion of a *contract not to be injured.* Although such a contract may indeed have been appropriate, the breach of contract claim referred to the more mundane contracts previously adverted to, including those for dormitory accommodation and university health services.

Harvard's limitation defence of the contract claim was, literally, nonsensical. It obviously fell on its own demerits. However, without granting a hearing, and without providing any reasons, the District Court had sustained it. The Court of Appeals in its judgment had failed even to refer to the contract claim.

Thus, a further unassailable ground for the granting of certiorari by the Supreme Court had been made out.

The final two of the nine grounds advanced to the Supreme Court for certiorari turned on the decisions of the Irish courts in the litigation, and the obligation on the American courts under international law to recognise them. Virtually all issues before the American courts in the case against Harvard had previously been litigated in Ireland between 1987 and 1992, and had been decided in my favour. Thus, in the previous case against University College Cork, in which Harvard had been a privy in interest, the Irish Supreme Court had unanimously decided on July 9, 1992, that I had become entitled to a pension by reason of the injuries sustained at Harvard in the last months of my employment with University College Cork.

Moreover, in the personal injuries case in Ireland against both Harvard and University College Cork, the High Court in 1992 had not considered the claim to be time barred. This finding had important estoppel-related implications for the American courts, since the limitations provisions in both Irish and Massachusetts law in relation to personal injuries are identical in most critical respects. In adjudicating on the case in 1992, the High Court had in fact ruled that the personal injuries case against Harvard should be pursued in the United States on the basis that it was the most convenient forum.

The above decision of the High Court was made on April 6, 1992, and was confirmed unanimously by the Supreme Court on June 19, 1992.

Under international law, the American courts had a clear obligation to recognise the findings of fact and law by the Irish High and Supreme courts in relation to the limitations issue as well as other pertinent issues in the litigation. That obligation arose under the long and well established principles of comity of nations and of courts. One of the requirements of same is that the courts of one state recognise the judicial decisions of another state.

The lower courts either ignored or blatantly sidetracked the Irish decisions in the litigation. The District Court had given no reasons for its decision. The Court of Appeals had disingenuously resorted to patently false propositions in order to avoid the international legal obligations to recognise the Irish decisions. Thus, for instance, its judgment incorrectly recited that:-

"The purported judgment of the Irish Supreme Court award-ing to plaintiff a pension from University College Cork is irrelevant to the issues before us. Harvard was not a party to the alleged Irish litigation."

Both statements are obviously false. Thus, first, the pension case against University College Cork turned on the same facts as the case against Harvard – both had arisen from the retaliatory abuse at Harvard in 1987.

Secondly, Harvard had clearly been a party to the Irish litigation. It had been a privy in interest with University College Cork in the pension case between 1987 and 1992.

In sum, in the petition to the Supreme Court, the grounds for certiorari that were based in international law were also fully substantiated.

29 Supreme Court Decision

Hard on the belated acknowledgment on January 18, 1995, by the clerk's office of the filing of the petition on Novem-ber 5, 1994, the Supreme Court denied certiorari on Feb-ruary 27, 1995. Notification came in the following letter:-

" SUPREME COURT OF THE UNITED STATES
OFFICE OF THE CLERK
WASHINGTON, D.C. 20533

February 27, 1995

Re: Denis Martin Linehan v. Harvard University
No. 94-7657

Dear Mr. Linehan:
The Court today entered the following order in the above enti-tled case:

The petition for a writ of certiorari is denied. Justice Breyer took no part in the consideration or decision of this petition.

Very truly yours,
William K. Suter, Clerk "

Both the denial, and the manner in which it was reached, seemed askew. Harvard had not even formally pleaded in the Supreme Court. No oral hearing had taken place. Apparent grounds existed on the basis of which at least one of the presiding judges should have disqualified himself by reason of bias. No reasons were given for the decision.

The decision disregarded the grounds that had been made out for certiorari. Most importantly, it perpetuated an injustice that was then longstanding for nearly eight years.

Because the court gave no reasons for its decision, one must proceed indirectly in seeking to identify the basis for it.

As already outlined, no less than three separate hurdles must be surmounted by a petitioner who seeks certiorari from the Supreme Court. First, grounds for same must be made out in fact and in law. Secondly, even where grounds have been established, the court retains a discretion under rule 10.1 to deny certiorari. Thirdly, in order to exercise its discretion in favour of granting certiorari, rule 10.1 provides that there must be *special and important reasons therefor.*

It is indisputable that the petition had overcome the first hurdle, i.e., that grounds for certiorari should be made out. It is highly significant in that regard that Harvard had not challenged the petition.

It is also indisputable that the petition had overcome the third hurdle for granting certiorari, i.e., that *special and important reasons* be established. Such reasons, as they are defined in rule 10.1(a), formed part of the petition.

By the foregoing process of elimination, the basis for the Supreme Court's denial of certiorari can be isolated. That basis can be summarised in one word, i.e., *discretion.*

The Supreme Court denied certiorari in the unexplained exercise of its discretion. The lack of explanation for the manner in which the discretion was exercised allows one to speculate in this regard. Did the Harvard connection in the court carry the day for the university? Was political influence exercised on the court to favour Harvard? These are two obvious lines of speculation.

Bias is an universally recognised basis upon which a judge – or indeed a juror – can be asked to disqualify himself in a case. Objectivity, impartiality and personal disinterest are prerequisites to the exercise of judicial office.

Challenges to a judge sitting in a case that are based on bias are normally made prior to the commencement of the hearing.

No less than five of the nine judges of the Supreme Court 1995 were Harvard *alumni*. These five included Chief Justice Rehnquist. On that basis alone, the issue of bias clearly arose in the context of the petition that was denied on February 27, 1995.

Because an oral hearing was also denied prior to that decision being made, the opportunity to challenge for bias was also denied.

Over and above the issue of bias that arose in the context of the Supreme Court, a dimension of *prejudice* against the case could be inferred from the overall pattern of dealing with the case throughout the entire federal judicial system. At virtually all stages, in the conflict between me and Harvard, the latter had in figurative terms been granted both the *inside track* and the *chequered flag*. Did this dimension of antipathy towards the case derive solely from the Harvard connection, or was it politicised in a more dispersed manner?

An identical question had arisen in the initial Irish phase of the litigation. In 1993, it had become a widely proven certainty that significant sections of the Irish bodies politic and bureaucratic were either implicated or acquiescent in the cover-up sought to be achieved on behalf of the dons of U.C.C. and Harvard. The question now under consideration is whether this phenomenon also existed in the United States.

How dispersed was the antipathy against the case in the federal justice system? Did the pattern of negativity represent official policy, as in Ireland? Because of the extent of the interactivity between Harvard and government in the United States such questions might reasonably not be expected to admit of clear-cut answers.

On the one hand, Harvard is a private corporation. Any one who has had any experience of dealing with it is likely to attest to its avid adherence to the profit motive. Most goods and services provided by Harvard are supplied at top-dollar rates. In view of same, Harvard's description of itself in its answer to the complaint as a *charitable institution* for purposes of seeking to limit its liability to pay compensation seems inappropriate. With a $3.5 billion endowment and a $650 million budget in 1986, Harvard is hardly a charity in the normal sense in which that expression is used.

Co-extensive with its private status, and its profit-oriented policies, Harvard's interactivity with government in the United States is such as to render it, in organic if not in formal terms, a type of adjunct to government. The cover story in Time magazine of September, 1986, delineated several facets of the relationship between Harvard and government. Two instances demonstrate the wide range of the interface. Thus, it was noted that:-

> "Six Presidents, from John Adams to John F. Kennedy, came from Harvard, bringing with them some potent Cambridge-bred notions and cronies. Franklin D. Roosevelt had his NEW DEAL, whose underlying Keynesianism, says Harvard Economist John Kenneth Galbraith, was imported from Cambridge. J.F.K. had his best and brightest, including Defense Secretary Robert McNamara and National Security Advisor McGeorge Bundy. Harvard's Henry Kissinger surely was the most powerful figure in the Nixon and Ford administrations."

Harvard's relationship with government has not been confined to the more obviously constitutional and democratic branches. It has also harboured and entertained the

C.I.A. The illegal activities of that organisation have caused it to be feared and detested both inside and outside the United States. The Time magazine article previously quoted from recounted the following episode that is indicative of Harvard's relationship with the C.I.A.:-

"[In 1985] *a mini-scandal at the Center of Middle Eastern Studies raised new questions about whether Government funding of university research might encroach on academic freedom. The center's director, professor Madav Safron, broke university policy by planning a conference on Islamic Fundamentalism without first notifying Harvard or participants that it had C.I.A. underwriting, and further offended colleagues by publishing a book on Saudi Arabia that contained no acknowledgement of similar financing."*

The question had arisen as to whether the treatment of the case by the courts substantiated a hypothesis that the policy to cover-up the abuse and injuries at Harvard in 1987 had formally extended beyond university circles and had in some way become governmental. Outlining and illustrating the osmotic relationship between Harvard and government in the United States may tend to support such a hypothesis, but does not prove its application in this case. However, in that regard, indisputable evidence had arisen in the period between March and May, 1987, when the retaliatory abuse and injuries at Harvard had been inflicted.

When the physical and overall agenda of abuse was not achieving the result required by the U.C.C. and Harvard dons, and after serious damage had been done to me, Harvard resorted to the Massachusetts Mediation Service.

"

MASSACHUSETTS MEDIATION SERVICE
Executive Office for Administration and Finance
12 Marshall Street, Boston, MA 02108 Tel: 617-727-2224

Denis Linehan   *May 5, 1987*
220 Holmes Hall
18 Everett Street
Cambridge, MA   02138
Dear Mr. Linehan:
*In accordance with our telephone conversation, I have enclosed
a copy of our brochure and our annual report.*

  *I look forward to talking with you on Tuesday, May 26 at 10
a.m. here at my office.*

                              Sincerely,
                              David O'Connor
DOC/fmr   *Executive Director*
Enclosures

MASSACHUSETTS
MEDIATION SERVICE

*This pamphlet describes the services, objectives and contributions
of a state office which resolves public disputes of statewide significance. The office provides information and independent mediators to help state agencies and private organizations improve
communication and formulate mutually satisfying agreements.*

  *Established in January 1985 by Secretary for Administra-
tion and Finance Frank T. Keefe, the Service seeks to increase
awareness of mediation among potential users in the state and
to increase opportunities for public officials to negotiate settle-
ments of disputes. The office is one of five such agencies operating in state government across the United States. "*

Partial funding for the Mediation Service is provided by the
National Institute for Dispute Resolution, a private foundation in Washington, D.C.; Madaleine Crohn, President
and William R.Drake, Deputy Director. This support is
gratefully appreciated.

The foregoing proves conclusively that Harvard had resorted to an agency of the state of Massachusetts at that time.

The following extract proves with greater specificity the linkage between Harvard personnel and the Massachusetts Mediation Service – Frank Sander is shown to have been on the board of advisors of that body.

"BOARD OF ADVISORS

Appointed by the Governor and the Attorney General, the Board is comprised of representatives from business, public interest groups and state government. The Board reviews and comments on major policy issues concerning the service on a regular basis.

Stephen Rosenfeld
Chairman
Chief Legal Counsel
Executive Department
Commonwealth of Massachusetts

Florence Rubin
Vice-Chair
Massachusetts Council for Public Justice, Inc.

Judge John Cratsley
Chief, Public Protection Bureau
Department of the Attorney General Commonwealth of Massachusetts

Russell Simpson, Esq.
Goodwin, Proctor & Hoar

John D. Crosier
Executive Director
Massachusetts Business Roundtable

Paul Lazzaro
General Management and Services Assoc., Inc.

Rudolf Pierce, Esq.
LeBoef, Lamb, Leiby & MacRae

Donald Polk
Executive Director
Urban League of Eastern Massachusetts

Frank E.A. Sander
Bussey Professor of Law, Harvard Law School

Edward Sullivan
Executive Director
Massachusetts Teachers Association

Lawrence Susskind
Professor,
Massachusetts Institute of Technology

Charles H.W. Foster
Adjunct Research Fellow
Energy and Environmental Policy
Center
John F. Kennedy School
of Government

Eric Van Loon
Undersecretary, Executive
Office of Economic Affairs
Commonwealth of Massachusetts

Marcia Greenbaum
President
Society of Professionals in Dispute Resolution

Staff
David L. O'Connor, Executive Director
Cordelia E. Kellett, Assistant to the Director
Consultant Mediators, assigned on a case-by-case basis "

As is clear from the sworn deposition of August 31, 1987, Frank Sander figured prominently in events during the critical period of March to May, 1987. A leading exponent of alternative methods of dispute resolution, including mediation, by May, 1987, Frank Sander also had a major personal interest in effecting a resolution through the official mediation service of the state of Massachusetts. That initiative failed at that time because, on May 10, 1987, I was confined to intensive care with a suspected heart attack and other injuries then unknown at The Malden Hospital, Massachusetts.

In sum, two states – the Republic of Ireland and Massachusetts – are indisputably identified with the Harvard and U.C.C. dons attempts to secure what amounts to a *free pardon* at my expense, and that of my family and friends – and also at the expense of the fundamental values that are enshrined in the constitutions of both states.

The part of the question under consideration that remains outstanding is whether Harvard and U.C.C. resorted to their almost instinctive networking strategy in order to garner the support of the American *federal* government for their attempted cover-up. Does the denial of an oral hearing in *any* federal court support an affirmative answer? Does the pattern of negative decisions in all federal courts, and the groundless refusal by the clerk's office of the Supreme Court to acknowledge the filing of the petition for a significant period, speak of formal federal government support for a cover-up for the dons? Was the denial of certiorari by the Supreme Court on February 27, 1995, in the face of the facts and the law, and based only on unexplained discretion, simply a confirmation of such support?

The above questions may seem rhetorical.

30 Petition for Rehearing

When Harvard law school was in court, the Irish and American legal systems were coming into perspective in a new light. In contrast with their vaunted image of purveyors of law and even justice on occasion, the spectre was emerging of elaborate props, theatrical in essence, manipulable by and for the few.

The latter perspective coincides with a view that is expressed at a cutting edge of legal philosophy. This is the critical legal studies movement that emerged in the 1970's. Thus, in the feature article of Time magazine of September, 1986, that marked Harvard's 350th anniversary, it was noted that:-

"The law school, meanwhile, is recovering from a guerrilla war among some of its faculty. On one side stand old-timers who teach law as a pure discipline, without value colorations.

Attacking them is a rebel cadre under the banner of Critical Legal Studies, a left-leaning doctrine that claims the law is no impartial instrument but serves principally, and in partisan fashion, to maintain the status quo in society. Beneath the spoken issues lies a suspicion that the law school may have become too inbred and is not as concerned with legal ethics as it should be."

The thrust of critical legal studies, namely, the partisan abuse of law, had a special twist in this litigation. In both the Irish and American legal systems, and in particular at their apexes, U.C.C. and Harvard had what amounted to that which in political parlance is referred to as *direct representation.* At the very least, they had what is referred to as the proverbial *friend in court.*

The Supreme Court rules contain a somewhat unusual provision that still offered the prospect of a remedy in the American legal system notwithstanding the denial of certiorari on February 27, 1995. Under rule 44.2, a petitioner could petition for a rehearing if intervening or substantial grounds not previously presented existed.

Such a petition was filed on March 24, 1995. In presenting what could transpire to be the last formal pleading in the American legal circuit in the litigation, namely, the petition for a rehearing, the ruminations already outlined crystallised.

The groundless refusals by the office of the clerk of the Supreme Court to acknowledge the filing of the petition between November 5, 1994, and January 18, 1995, were highly significant.

"The original Petition was filed on November 5, 1994, but this was acknowledged only on January 18, 1995, after Notice Parties were introduced .... In the interim, the Petition had been blatantly stonewalled on the basis of a number of absurd and obviously unfounded reasons by the Clerk's Office."

From 1987 onwards, the primary objective of Harvard and U.C.C. relative to the litigation had been to keep their treasuries intact.

"Harvard and U.C.C. dons have pursued the objective of "killing this case quietly," by any means since 1987. A principal corollary of this is to achieve a cheap fix for their treasuries at my expense...."

One of the most bizarre aspects of the passage of the case

through the American federal judicial system is that neither I, nor Harvard, nor counsel on behalf of either party, ever appeared in open court. The requirement of due process had been put on ice in order to offset media attention.

> *"The Due Process clauses of the American Constitution, the Supreme Court Rules, international law and general jurisprudence all prescribe an oral hearing as an almost invariable feature of the common law adversarial system....*
>
> *The denial of same has worked a radical re-definition of Due Process in the American judicial system."*

Two universal requirements of natural justice are that reasons be given for judicial decisions, and that judges obviously be impartial. The petition for the rehearing took issue on both counts:-

> *"....Even from the limited standpoint of the present Petition, the failure to give reasons is clearly prejudicial. It has introduced an element of "shadow-boxing;" except by proceeding indirectly, one cannot challenge a decision for which no reasons have been given.*
>
> *....Even at this stage, I do not know which Justices made the decision entered on February 27 last. Obviously, therefore, I had no opportunity to challenge any of them from dealing with the case on the basis of bias."*

The fifth and sixth reasons advanced for the petition concerned the restriction of the pleadings and the failure of the court to take the obvious implication from Harvard's failure to plead.

A seventh reason for a rehearing focused on justice.

The closing submissions in the petition for rehearing compared the outcomes in relation to the litigation in both the Irish and American Supreme Courts.

> *"....Unless certiorari is granted in a rehearing, the American legal system will effectively "mirror" the Irish one in this case. Although very much a matter of "locking the stable door after the horse has bolted," what is termed the Irish legal system is also effectively fully compromised in this litigation."*

Whatever the outcome of the petition for rehearing, the decision of the Supreme Court would only be a terminal. If a rehearing were granted, that would simply offer the prospect of justice in an American court at another time. Otherwise, a forum outside both the American and Irish legal systems would need to be sought.

31 Final Decision of American Supreme Court

The final decision of the Supreme Court in the case against Harvard was given on April 24, 1995. The court denied certiorari.

SUPREME COURT OF THE UNITED STATES
OFFICE OF THE CLERK
WASHINGTON, D.C. 20543

April 24, 1995

> *Re:*   *Denis Martin Linehan*
> *v. Harvard University*
> *No. 94-7657*

Dear Mr. Linehan:
The Court today entered the following order in the above entitled case:

The petition for rehearing is denied. Justice Breyer took no part in the consideration or decision of this petition.

Very truly yours,
William K. Suter, Clerk.

Harvard had not been required to plead before the court. No oral hearing had taken place. No reasons for the denial of certiorari were given.

The denial of the petition for rehearing meant that no further means of legal redress against Harvard existed in the American legal system.

Objectively, in retrospect, the action against Harvard in the American legal system could be described, at a minimum, as a predictable *uphill battle*. Realistically, it could be characterised as more akin to an attempt to scale a glacier wearing roller-skates.

The 1995 American Supreme Court was a decidedly conservative one. Its effectively right wing majority consisted of Chief Justice William H. Rehnquist and Associate Justices Antonin Scalia, Clarence Thomas, Anthony M. Kennedy and Sandra Day O'Connor. Of these, Justices Kennedy and O'Connor are sometimes perceived as the more moderate of the conservatives.

The liberal bloc of the court consisted of Stephen G. Breyer, Ruth Bader Ginsburg, David H. Souter and John Paul Stevens. Two of these liberal-leaning justices, Ginsburg and Breyer, had been appointed by president Bill Clinton.

Such consolations as had been received from the court in the case against Harvard had come from members of the liberal bloc. Associate Justice Souter, in July, 1995, had extended the time for filing the petition for certiorari. Moreover, Associate Justice Breyer had taken no part in the consideration or the decision of the petition.

Viewed from another perspective, the 1995 Supreme Court might also have been predicted as predisposed towards deciding in favour of Harvard - no less than five of its members were *alumni* of Harvard. These were :- Chief Justice Rehnquist, and Associate Justices Kennedy, Scalia, Ginsburg and Souter.

I had proceeded in the Supreme Court *in forma pauperis*, a fact that suggests that my petition for certiorari came into the bailiwick of Chief Justice Rehnquist. In *The Brethren, Inside the Supreme Court*, a 1979 book by a Washington Post team that examines the behind-the-scenes working of the Supreme Court, it is noted that the Office of the Chief Justice was responsible for such petitions.

In 1973, at the law school of the university of Michigan, at Ann Arbor, I had attended a meeting at which Justice Rehnquist was the main speaker. At that time, the Watergate scandal was *going down* in the United States and, as an appointee of president Nixon, Justice Rehnquist had received a somewhat hostile reception from several of the other attendees at the meeting.

Bob Woodward and Scott Armstrong, a Washington Post team and authors of *The Brethren*, leave the reader in little doubt that Justice Rehnquist's establishment credentials were, in a sense, impeccable from an early time:-

> "*Richard Kleindienst, the Department Attorney General, had brought him to Washington in 1968 to serve as Assistant General to advise the department on legal strategy. He had performed brilliantly for the administration - justifying its anticrime measures, its tapping of domestic radicals,and the mass arrests during the previous spring's demonstrations. Rehnquist might have done his job too well. He might run into fire from congressional liberals. Blacks also seemed certain to oppose his nomination. Rehnquist had testified against a Phoenix civil rights act as recently as 1964, and in favour of limited school desegregation in 1967*".

As an associate justice on the Supreme Court, Rehnquist was equally predictable. Thus, according to Woodward and Armstrong, the liberals on the Supreme Court in 1971:-

> "*weren't surprised when Rehnquist began promptly to live up to his advance billing as a solid conservative vote, siding invariably with the prosecution in criminal cases, with business in antitrust cases, with employers in labour cases and with the government in speech cases*".

Rehnquist's Harvard associations are also adverted to in *The Brethren*. The authors note that:-

> "*Rehnquist was remarkably unstuffy. He thought it funny that there was a Rehnquist Club at Harvard Law School in which the leader was called the "Grand Rehnquisitor", and a weekly discussion called the Rehnquisition*".

In preparing my application to the Supreme Court, I had been initially surprised by the rarity of applications to that court that succeeded. On the basis of reported Supreme Court decisions, it appeared to me that the overwhelming majority of applications were unsuccessful. That impression is in fact borne out by statistics given in *The Brethren* relating to I.F.P.'s, this being the working acronym used with respect to in *forma pauperis* petitions.

The statistics quoted by Woodward and Armstrong confirm that the vast majority of I.F.P.'s are likely to be viewed with some scepticism and to get short shrift:-

"These petitions constituted the bulk of the approximately five thousand that come to the court each year. They were called in forma pauperis petitions, or "I.F.P's." The Court got only one copy of each, rather than the forty that were required of those able to pay. Most of the "I.F.P's" were from prisoners who alleged a violation of their constitutional rights. All the justices agreed that only a few petitions had merit, but Burger thought that all I.F.P's were a waste of time. In a 1965 Court of Appeals opinion (Williams v. U.S.), he had denounced the "Disneyland" contentions of those who had been found guilty and were still trying to get out of jail by raising technical objections."

My experience in the Supreme Court, and my reflections thereafter, have been illuminating. As a graduate student at Michigan and Harvard, I had been presented with and received an *upbeat* view of American law and legal institutions. When I ceased paying my university fees, and became a consumer of the legal services that I had studied, I found that the reality did not match - or even resemble - that which I had been educated about. As an experienced academic and practising lawyer, I had expected some discrepancy between the *law in the books* and the *law in action*. I had not however been prepared for the yawning chasm that I found to exist between them.

My experiences in the Irish and American legal systems have undoubtedly alienated me from both, and served to roll-back over a quarter century of what I now view essentially as misleading indoctrination - *virtual reality*, one might say. While both the need for and the value of positive legal systems are indisputable, their limitations and openness to abuse have been indelibly impressed on me.

Whether in the particular case, or in the general one, Juvenal's ancient question remains - namely, *quis custodiet ipsos custodes?* - Who is to guard the guards themselves?

32 Washington D.C. to Cork, via Dublin

A first version of this book was launched on May 13, 1995, some two weeks after I was notified of the American Supreme Court decision. One week later, on May 20, 1995, at about 11 p.m. on Saturday evening, I was arrested by three members of the Irish police, who trespassed in the garden of my home. After physical abuse, I was imprisoned in Cork prison for an alleged failure to display a tax disc in February, 1994, fifteen months previously.

The initial charge of the alleged failure to display a tax disc had been made by affixing a notice to my car at about fifteen minutes before midnight on Sunday, February, 27, 1994. The car was parked outside my home at the time, which is in a quiet suburban estate, off the main road, and in a poorly lit area. By reason of its condition, the car had not been legally liable to tax.

The circumstances of the police activity at that time almost irrefutably point to special surveillance.

The District Court conviction for the alleged tax disc offence had been made in my absence on November 10, 1994. I filed appeal papers thereafter. At Cork Circuit Court, on November 29, 1995, the District Court conviction was quashed. Thus, there had never been a sustainable legal basis for the assault, arrest and imprisonment on May 20, 1995. In any event, the warrant used to effect the arrest was invalid - it had been both issued and purported to be executed several months outside the legal time limits.

At the time of my arrest on May 20, 1995, threats of further police harassment and intimidation were made.

I went on hunger strike while in Cork prison until my release on Tuesday, May 23, 1995, after an application to the District Court. On my return home, items of personal property, a stereo unit and tape were found to be missing.

I complained these latest human rights violations to the European Commission on Human Rights, on July 28, 1995 - I had previously complained to that Commission in 1992. I also reported the matter to the Human Rights Committee of the United Nations on September 5, 1995.

My arrest on May 20, 1995, occurred in the context of a wider range of inimical activity by American and Irish state bodies as the following timetable proves:
TIMETABLE

(i) April 24 : The U.S. Supreme Court denied certiorari. Notification came at the end of April.

The Supreme Court had been aware of the forthcoming book, and would have had an interest in preventing its publication because of the irregularities disclosed in relation to the court's dealing with the case. In retrospect, it is reasonable to infer that the decision of the U.S. Supreme Court appears to have triggered a bizarre, extraordinary and unlawful chain of activity in relation to me in the weeks following in Ireland.

The U.S. Supreme Court decision would of course have been known to university administrators, their political allies, their affiliates in the Irish civil service, and to their legal advisers.

(ii) May 5 : An opposition spokesperson tabled a parliamentary question on the failure of the attorney general's office to reply over a period of about five months to correspondence from a Belfast solicitor, Ted Lavery, in a case involving substantial compensation.

(iii) May 9 : Ted Lavery received a faxed letter to his

Belfast office *expressing "regret"* at the delay in replying to his correspondence.

(iv) May 10 : I was sent a demand for possession of my
house from Cork Corporation, in respect of alleged
arrears of mortgage for which an insurance company
had accepted liability in 1990.

(v) May 13 : A first version of this book was launched.

(vi) May 15 : I received a letter on behalf of Dermot
Gleeson, attorney general, *expressing "regret" at the five
(5) month delay in replying to a letter dated December 23,
1994,* and disclaiming a function in the matter raised
therein. My letter of December 23, 1994, had raised the
issues of costs arising under the Supreme Court Order
of July 9, 1992, and also of compensation from Harvard
and U.C.C.

(vii) May 20 : I was unlawfully arrested, abused and
jailed in Cork prison for a wrongfully alleged offence
of failure to display a tax disc in 1994.

(viii) May 30 : Matt Russell, senior legal assistant in the
attorney general's office, was compelled to resign for
errors in dealing with letters from Ted Lavery, solicitor. Matt Russell was formerly a law professor at Trinity College, and was a member of the Kildare Street
University Club.

The Irish prime minister, John Bruton, noted that Matt
Russell's retirement was *closing the book* on criticisms of the
attorney general's office. However, no reference was made
to my correspondence. Moreover, although it was widely
reported that Dermot Gleeson, attorney general, had con-
flicts of interest in some ten to twelve cases, all of these
were not publicly identified. An obvious question that arises is whether my litigation with Harvard and University
College Cork was - and remains - one of such cases.

Between 1987 (the year of the injuries sustained at Har-
vard) and 1992 (the year of the success in the Irish Supreme
Court in the litigation with University College Cork, with
Harvard as an interest party), and indeed after 1992 in

relation to costs of more than £¹/₄ million (including interest) under the Supreme Court Order of July 9, 1992, there had occurred a persistent abuse of the civil processes in the legal system on behalf of university interests in litigation where it is reasonable to infer that Dermot Gleeson had at least a consultative role.

During 1995 - in May and November - there had occurred serious abuses of the criminal processes in the legal system against me. The police, the prison system and the Cork state solicitor's office had been abused in that period.

This had occurred in the months following on Dermot Gleeson's appointment as attorney general.

After I was taken inside Cork prison, two of the police engaged in verbal abuse and intimidation. Garda McCarthy, the driver of the car, in front of his colleagues and a prison officer, described me as an "asshole".

The sergeant in the arrest team, Pat Hayes, before leaving the prison, approached me and stated that: - *"There will be more Saturday nights like this."*

He stated this with assurance, in such a way that confirmed the interpretation of the entire events of the evening - he and his colleagues, including Garda Dunlea, were operating under a mandate from an *authority* that, or who, was perceived as being outside and above the law.

The eventual outcome of the appeal, against the conviction on which the arrest and imprisonment were purportedly based, gave a legal underpinning to the hypothesis that the arrest and imprisonment had been intended to get me out of the way at the time in question - i.e., the United States Supreme Court decision in the case against Harvard, the launch of the first edition of this book that set out the irregularities in that court's dealing with the case, and the surfacing in the Dail and media about delays in the Irish attorney general's office in dealing with correspondence relating to litigation.

The parallelism between events in May, 1995, and those of March to May, 1987, is noteworthy. In 1987, shortly after my first case against U.C.C. in the Irish courts, I was assaulted at my residence within Harvard by security elements. In 1995, shortly after my case against Harvard in the American courts, I was again assaulted by security elements, on this occasion at my home in Ireland. The same gang was operating, using the same methods.

Hate-filled cowards, they inevitably sought to operate by proxy. Based in the administrations of U.C.C. and Harvard, with the vast treasuries of these institutions at their disposal, and granted virtual immunity by the national courts, for them it was nearly a perfect war.

33 New World Order

The service of a *trumped-up* copy summons on November 3, 1995, was suggestive of a new, much more serious and ruthless type of state action being exercised against me on behalf of and by the Harvard and U.C.C. dons and their affiliates in the Irish legal system. As a pointer to who the clandestine power brokers are, it is significant that once again - as in May, 1995, - the November, 1995, abuses entailed a manipulation of the criminal processes in the legal system.

Dermot Gleeson, attorney general, and Michael Mortell, U.C.C. president, remained in close association at this time. On November 10, 1995, both met at the law society dinner within U.C.C.

In October, 1995, I received notification that my appeal against the alleged offence of non-display of a tax disc on February 27, 1994, was listed for Cork Circuit Court on November 29, 1995.

On November 3, 1995, the sergeant in the arrest team of May 20, 1995 returned to my home. On this occasion, he served a copy summons on me in respect of the evening of May 20, 1995.

The thrust of the copy summons was that, under the influence of alcohol, I had been disorderly on the night of my wrongful arrest, and that I had wrongfully resisted arrest.

The reference to alcohol was itself extraordinary because, since December, 1993, I had been a certified pioneer! This signifies a formal pledge to abstain from alcohol. An order was being sought to bind me to the peace in respect of all persons, although I am a committed pacifist with no record of violence. Such a request in the summons was clearly invidious - if granted, it would open the door for entrapment at any time in the future.

The summons was set down for hearing at Cork District Court on November 24, 1995 - such that three weeks only had been received to allow preparation for the hearing.

The strategy was clear - at short notice, I was subjected to criminal proceedings in two different courts, in the space of six days, at the end of November, 1995.

In addition, on November 16, 1995, I was subjected at short notice to a third hearing in Cork District Court at the suit of Telecom Eireann, a state monopoly company, in respect of an alleged telephone bill of about £700. This sum had previously been proved in the High Court against University College Cork by another party. It is noteworthy that, at this time, Michael Lowry, as minister for transport, energy and communications, had responsibility for Telecom. One year later, in November, 1996, Lowry was forced from government after it was revealed that the substantial costs of an extension to his house had been paid by Dunnes Stores Ltd., a supermarket chain to which he supplied goods and services. This disclosure led to the establishment of the payments to politicians tribunal in 1997, but did not prevent Lowry from topping the poll in his Tipperary North constituency in the general election held on June 6, 1997.

To put it in perspective, while owed more than a quarter million pounds by a state funded body, University College Cork, under a Supreme Court Order of July 9, 1992, I was being sued for about £700 claimed and proved by another party under that order.

Harvard and University College Cork clearly had friends in high places in the Irish civil service - and, clearly, they were using them.

On November 16, 1995, the Telecom Eireann case was adjourned. Telecom was represented by Barry Galvin, Cork state solicitor, who had no less than five witnesses in court.

On November 17, 1995, I applied to Cork District Court to issue summonses against the police who had arrested me on May 20, 1995, and who were parties to the further summonses served on November 3, 1995.

On November 18, 1995, a Saturday, at a specially arranged sitting of Cork District Court, before judge Terence Finn, I made a complaint under oath in respect of the charges proffered by me.

At this hearing, it was conveyed that the alcohol-related charge was not contained on the original summons. By dint of some circumstance, this charge - that is part of a standard package of related charges - had been decipherable only on the copy summons.

On November 23, 1995, the remaining charges came initially before judge U. MacRuairc, who declined to hear this case also by reason of his acquaintance with me. These charges were of course highly anomalous. They were brought arising out of an unlawful arrest, assault and imprisonment - *prosecute the victim* was the bizarre logic of the charges. The case was transferred to another judge, Mr. Early. The director of public prosecutions was represented by inspector Crockett of Togher police station. Four police witnesses were in attendance. Thus, in an eight day period, between the Telecom and D.P.P. cases, no less than nine witnesses from the state and semi-state sectors were brought to court against me.

During the course of the hearing, Judge Early directed that the tape recording of the proceedings by my stenographer should cease. To the point that such recording was standard practice in the High and Supreme Courts, Judge Early said *"not in this court"*. After a variety of applications, the trial was adjourned to enable application to the High Court.

Moreover, in a critical decision, at Cork Circuit Court, on November 29, 1995, Judge Moran upheld the appeal against the District Court conviction of November 10, 1994, for non-display of a tax disc. The implications of this were far-reaching. For instance, it established that there had been no legally sustainable basis for the arrest and imprisonment on May 20, 1994.

It is clear that the prolonged and concentrated attacks by state agencies in 1995 stemmed from the litigation against U.C.C. and Harvard. That litigation had given rise to a true Orwellian scenario in which multiple state agencies had been abused since 1987. These agencies included: - the revenue commissioners, the chief state solicitor's office, the High Court taxing master's office, Cork Corporation, Telecom Eireann, the Cork state solicitors office, the police, the courts and the prison system.

U.C.C. and Harvard had used their financial resources and their political and civil service connections on a mission of suppression and destruction. An escalation of the destruction processes occurred in May and November, 1995, with unlawful resort to the criminal law processes - police and prison system.

The November, 1995, furore had hardly subsided when a further negative-control type offensive was made. On January 31, 1996, University College Cork ceased in all respects to comply with the Supreme Court Order of July 9, 1992. My monthly pension was stopped without notice. Neither Michael Mortell, U.C.C. president, nor Michael Kelleher, U.C.C. secretary, were available to explain the latest contempt of court, that was obviously designed as a further suppressive measure. The cheque was paid on February 1, 1996, after the publication of a submission on the abuses to a parliamentary sub-committee.

The failed offensive by U.C.C. was a salutary reminder of the economic dimension of the urban warfare that was ongoing, as well as of its university *situs*.

34 Low Lying Cunning

Both the range of hostilities against me in Ireland from 1987 onwards, and the personnel involved, pointed conclusively to Irish governmental involvement in the attempted university cover-up on foot of the retaliatory abuse with a sonic device at Harvard between March and May, 1987.

Irish state agencies and personnel had again mounted a series of offensives, concentrated in May, 1995, in the immediate aftermath of the American Supreme Court's quixotic disposition of my case against Harvard on April 24, 1995. A further series of offensives had been concentrated in the November, 1995, period.

One would need to be an astute and well informed observer to appreciate the diverse and low key range of hostile activities that was being orchestrated and connived in. The statistics speak for themselves.

Controllers of the Irish legal system were pursuing a policy of a concentrated, low visibility pressure campaign that was also draining my financial resources and wasting my time. This was obviously in the interests of U.C.C., Harvard and their government affiliates.

A significant breakthrough came on April 17, 1996. By letter of that date, I was informed that the European Commission on Human Rights had registered my complaint against the Irish state. The complaint was being registered retrospectively to July 28, 1995, unless the European Commission should decide otherwise.

International recognition was being given to the evidence that had been furnished of human rights violations. This recognition was being afforded under the aegis of the regime established by the European Convention on Human Rights.

The European Convention on Human Rights is a treaty whereby the thirty four nations belonging to the council of Europe secure certain fundamental rights. The European Commission on Human Rights is the administrative body within the European human rights regime.

The Commission may also refer the petition to the European Court of Human Rights. That court had adjudicated in 1978 on a case that arose from sonic abuse, *inter alia.* In that case, Ireland had been the plaintiff, and the United Kingdom had been the defendant. The court, like the Commission, is based in Strasbourg.

Complaints to the European Commission on Human Rights are not registered automatically. After the complaint was made on July 28, 1995, extensive proofs were submitted in both January and February, 1996, before the complaint was ultimately registered on April 16, 1966. At that point, the commission had available to it considerable evidence of the abuses by Irish state agencies on foot of the attempted cover-up of the sonic abuse at Harvard in 1987.

Before the commission could adjudicate on the complaint, however, it would need to be *admitted.* This second stage bears *inter alia* on the jurisdiction of the commission to reach a decision. Based on the statistics for the years 1955-1991, only about 1 in 17 complaints is admitted by the commission. This low admission rate, in combination with a waiting period of up to five years for an adjudication by the European Court of Human Rights, means that the protection for human rights afforded by the institutions based in Strasbourg is, at best, threadbare. On registration of the complaint, I was informed by letter dated April 17, 1996, that:-

". . . a single member of the Commission, acting as Rapporteur, will carry out a preliminary examination of this application and report to the Commission on the question of its admissibility."

Further proofs of the abuses by Irish state agencies were furnished by me to the commission on February 21, 1997. Shortly thereafter, by letter of March 20, 1997, I was informed that a committee of three members - G. Jorundsson, J.-C. Geus and C. Birsan - had deemed my complaint inadmissible after private deliberations on February 27, 1997. This decision was tersely communicated:-

COUNCIL OF EUROPE   CONSEIL DE L'EUROPE

EUROPEAN COMMISSION OF HUMAN RIGHTS

". . . the Committee
DECLARES THE APPLICATION INADMISSIBLE."

Thus, nineteen months after the complaint had been introduced - and with no evidence of the commission having acted on it in that period - an almost instantaneous decision of inadmissibility was reached after the third set of proofs was furnished in February, 1997. These proofs identified pivotal figures in the Irish political and legal establishment who were complicit in the abuses. They had also reiterated the American interest in the matter. Thus, the proofs included the following letter of support from Mr. Edward Kennedy, U.S. senator for Massachusetts:-

"EDWARD M. KENNEDY
MASSACHUSETTS

United States Senate

WASHINGTON, DC 20510-2101

December 23, 1996

Mr. Denis M. Linehan
Legal Advice & Consultancy Services

22 Summerstown Grove
Wilton, Cork
Ireland

Dear Mr. Linehan:

Thank you very much for sending to me the information about the book you are publishing regarding your case before the European Commission on Human Rights. I appreciate you sending me the pages mentioning my involvement with the situation.

If there is anything more I can do to assist you, please do not hesitate to contact my office. I am happy to offer you my best wishes in this endeavor.

> *Sincerely*
> *Edward M. Kennedy*

2400 JFK Federal Building
Boston, MA 02203   "

Senator Kennedy's correspondence was but one of a number of positive letters I received in late 1996 from prominent politicians who had read extracts from a previous book on the litigation, *And Nothing But the Truth*. I also received such letters from Fianna Fáil deputy leader, Mary O'Rourke, dated November 19, 1996, and from Fianna Fáil's David Andrews, dated November 21, 1996.

Faced with a complaint that bore on matters arising in the United States as well as in Ireland, the commission had refused to take jurisdiction. It bears emphasis that this decision did not go to the merits of the complaint, but only to its admissibility. Whereas one cannot be definitive in concluding what was the primary consideration in the minds of the three more or less anonymous committee members who had deliberated in private, it is reasonable to infer that, as in the 1992 complaint, the key factor had been the involvement of Harvard. By letter dated June 25, 1992, from the secretariat of the commission, I had been informed that:-

"... Harvard University does not fall within the jurisdiction of Ireland or any other Council of Europe Member State. It would seem therefore that any application from you would have little prospect of success."

This conclusion is verified by the committee's attitude towards the evidence available as to state abuses. The last paragraph of my covering letter of February 21, 1997, to the commission read as follows:-

"... I am presently preparing further evidence (including tapes and photographs), and will forward these as soon as possible."

The commission was not prepared to consider that evidence. It debarred itself from receiving it by deeming the complaint inadmissible.

New world order forces are shaping the modern world. My personal experiences in the previous decade suggested that my fate had been significantly affected by proponents of same. Although new world order politics are far advanced, the downside of their implications is concealed as a matter of routine. In fact, control of the media and other channels of communication is a basic strategy of the secretive type of government that is entailed.

However, the record of the conflict between 1985 and 1996 contained numerous indications that a distinctive new world order exercise was in train. New world order forces are commonly identified, not simply with governments, but with universities that serve as recruitment and conditioning grounds for personnel that will promote the single world government objective. Harvard's foreign graduate programs have been publicly identified in the past with CIA infiltration.

The physical and psychological abuses between March and May, 1987, at Harvard, had not been conducted by academics in their intervals between lectures. The probability is that they were exercised by members of the numerous security forces that mingle in the Harvard community.

These forces overtly include Harvard's private police, and the Cambridge City police. More covertly, they include CIA and FBI personnel.

In sum, my successful High Court action in 1986 against U.C.C. had brought me into conflict with both the Irish and American establishments in the following decade. The experience has changed me. Like Paul on the road to Damascus, I came to see the light. I had been keeping very bad company.

The registration of my complaint by the European Commission on Human Rights did not deter the U.C.C. and Harvard factions from their abusive actions. Accordingly, on November 25, 1996, I applied to the High Court to stay in the Irish courts proceedings that were the subject of the complaint registered by the commission.

The avid and continuing interest of U.C.C. and Harvard was again clearly demonstrated at this time. The High Court in Dublin is dispersed through numerous chambers, between several floors, over a wide area of the Four Courts building. My application on November 25, 1996, was down for hearing towards the end of the list in one of the more remote upstairs chambers. Nevertheless, no less than three former members of U.C.C. law faculty from the critical period between 1985 and 1987 found cause to be in that court on that day. Two of these - Pat Horgan, B.L., and John White, S.C. - were long time associates of Bryan McMahon, solicitor. John White, moreover, was a graduate of Harvard law school. Both had actively participated in the attempted cover-up since 1987.

By and large, members of U.C.C. and Harvard law faculties who had any type of interest in effecting a cover-up had stayed at two or three removes from the actual proceedings in court after 1987. Any witness summonses served on them were routinely evaded. Moreover, they had nearly always found it possible to engage other lawyers either to represent their interests, or to conduct a watching brief on their behalf. This disciplined and cautious low profile approach had served them well for many years.

Accordingly, the presence of Pat Horgan and John White in the remote upstairs chambers of the High Court on November 25, 1996, when university interests were in issue, was a remarkable departure from a longstanding formula.

The fact that the history of abuses by U.C.C. and Harvard had passed out of both the Irish and American jurisdictions would obviously have alarmed the universities. This, combined with the prospect of a stay on the use of the legal national machinery to damage or discredit me - such as was contemplated on November 25, 1996 - could have been interpreted by interested parties as marking, for them, the beginning of the end. One could understand how certain of them might, uncharacteristically, abandon their studied caution in order to assess developments at first hand.

Ultimately, on February 3, 1997, the High Court refused to stay in the Irish courts proceedings that were under the jurisdiction of the European Commission. It also refused to refer the issues of community law that arose to the Court of Justice for a preliminary ruling under Article 177 of the Treaty of Rome.

Prominent members of the Irish legal system were implicated in the cover-up attempts and the attendant abuses. The High Court decision of February 3, 1997, in effect condoned the continuation of these abuses and also withheld the case from the scrutiny of the Court of Justice of the European Union. The High Court decision was appealed to the Supreme Court on March 3, 1997. As a court of last resort, the Supreme Court is obliged under Article 177 of the Treaty of Rome to refer issues of community law that arise for a preliminary ruling. Thus, if it did not stay the internal abuses - such as the continued withholding of costs now estimated at about £1/3 million, and the *keel-hauling* through the courts - these would be referred to another international legal system apart from the regime established by the European Convention of Human Rights.

The potential to have my case examined by a second international legal system stemmed from Article F(2) of the Treaty on European Union, i.e., the Maastricht Treaty of 1993. That provision reads as follows:-

"The Union shall respect fundamental rights, as guaranteed by the European Convention for the Protection of Human Rights and Fundamental Freedoms."

This short, recent and little known provision has enormous potential for the advancement of human rights in Europe. Many countries who have ratified the European Convention of Human Rights have not specifically incorporated it into their national legal systems. In such countries, including Ireland and the United Kingdom, the European Convention has existed only in a limbo-like state - persuasive, perhaps, but without the force of law. In the specific case, its guarantees are apt to be found to be illusory.

At its face value, Article F(2) of the Maastricht Treaty has altered that condition in states that are members of the European Union. In such countries, Article F(2) has *direct effect* as community law.

U.C.C., Harvard and their allies in government had been taken unawares when the European Commission on Human Rights registered my complaint in 1995. The cover-up had gone from their control. My initiatives based on Article F(2) of Maastricht added greatly to their discomfiture, as the prospects of having the long history of abuses examined and censured by the institutions of the European Union meant that they now had to carry the war to other international agencies apart from the European Commission of Human Rights.

The initiatives under Maastricht started to bear fruit in early 1997. In March, 1997, I was informed that the Commission of the European Union, that is based in Brussels, had registered my complaint. More or less contemporaneously, it was also entered in the register of petitions of the European Parliament, that is based in Luxembourg. The cover-up had begun to disintegrate.

In the Irish courts, also, at this time, legal representatives of the interests of U.C.C. and Harvard were being challenged in respect of their behaviour in other matters. For instance, Dermot Gleeson, attorney general, was subpoenaed to the High Court on March 20, 1997, in order that his role be examined in a debacle where sixteen persons were imprisoned by an improperly constituted court. Gleeson did not comply with the subpoena, on the basis that there was no relevant evidence he could give that would not be privileged.

This type of evasion of legal process no longer surprised me. I had seen it used repeatedly by the university clique since 1986. The judicial response also had become predictable - they tended to *play along* with the dodging.

Mine is not the only litigation in which there was a resort to diabolical legal tactics during the tenure of the rainbow coalition government that ended on May 15, 1997. That government was also aptly accused of thuggery and terrorism by the opposition in the case of the late Brigid McCole. The latter, one of several recipients of contaminated blood products from the blood transfusion service board, died in October, 1996. Lawyers for the board had admitted liability to Mrs. McCole. However, while she was on her death bed, the board warned Mrs. McCole that it would pursue her for costs, as far as the Supreme Court if necessary, if she refused to settle and pursued a case for aggravated damages. The threat had struck fear into the heart of the dying woman. Her family succeeded in gaining the support of a number of politicians, including Brian Cowen of Fianna Fáil.

Michael Buckley, chief state solicitor, infuriated the opposition in early May, 1997, by refusing to appear before the parliamentary committee on social affairs to account for the legal strategy adopted in the case. He relied on the doctrine of separation of powers, and was supported in this by Dermot Gleeson, whose term as attorney general ended with that of the government on May 15, 1997. The latter, on his own behalf and that of his clients, has repeatedly excelled himself as a type of artful dodger. In my experience, it is not an art that is conducive either to due accountability or to justice.

35 All Eyes on the Money

The payment to politicians tribunal was set up on February 7, 1997, to inquire into and report on payments from either Ben Dunne or Dunne's Stores Ltd to politicians. It began its public sittings on April 21, 1997. The legal backdrop to the tribunal included the Prevention of Corruption Acts, 1889 to 1916, a range of taxation on income and gifts, and the Ethics in Public Office Act, 1995. However, Mr. Justice Brian McCracken, a highly respected judge, stressed at the outset that no criminality or wrong-doing was being alleged against anyone appearing before the tribunal.

Speculation was rife prior to the public sittings of the tribunal that Charles Haughey, former prime minister, had received substantial largesse from Ben Dunne. Haughey had already denied this, for instance, in letters dated November 14, 1994, to the solicitors for Dunne's Stores Ltd, and dated March 7, 1997, to the tribunal. Thus, the tribunal sittings began dramatically with the evidence given by Ben Dunne that he had *handed* £210,000 to Haughey at the latter's home in 1991. The payment consisted of three drafts for £70,000 each made payable to fictitious payees. The drafts showed up in the same bank account as four other payments Dunne said he had made to Haughey. The total of the five payments was £1.3 million. No political favour was asked for or received in connection with these payments, which were made to assist Haughey in his financial difficulties.

Ben Dunne, who was represented by Noel Smyth, solicitor, also testified that he had made other payments to Michael Lowry, apart from the cost of extending his home. Disclosure of the latter had brought about Lowry's retirement from the government in November, 1996, and had led to the setting up of the tribunal. Lowry was represented by Donal O'Donnell, S.C. O'Donnell had been part of the legal front team that had served the interests of U.C.C. and Harvard in my litigation. He had also acted for the Goodman interests with Dermot Gleeson, S.C., in the beef tribunal. The total of their respective fees from same had been over £1.5 million.

Inflated reports of the payments by Ben Dunne to Michael Lowry in the Irish Times and by RTE on April 22, 1997, were corrected by O'Donnell on April 23. The evidence given was that Lowry had been paid £155,000 and, in addition, £34,000 for Christmas bonuses. Mr. Justice McCracken, the sole member of the tribunal, agreed that the media reporting had been unfair and inaccurate. He emphasised the need for great accuracy about the sums involved.

Mr. Dunne stated that all money paid to Mr. Lowry was part of the business arrangement between their respective companies. No political favour was asked for or received in connection with the payments.

The payments to Haughey and Lowry were not unique. For instance, Dunne testified that he had given £185,000 to the Fine Gael party, £15,000 to the Labour party and £7,000 to a local branch of the Fianna Fáil party. John Bruton, leader of Fine Gael, had received £2,500 in respect of constituency activities. Dick Spring, Labour party leader, had obtained £50,000 on behalf of a tourist project in his constituency. Numerous other payments were recounted. All had stemmed from Mr. Dunne's magnanimity. No political favour was asked for or received in connection with the largesse.

The sense of a political system awash with undisclosed private funding was unmistakable. An Irish Times editorial of April 23, 1997, commented that:-

"Mr. Dunne was to the main political parties a sort of money pump to which they felt they could have recourse as and when funds began to run low."

It also touched on the larger point, namely, that the Dunne payments represented only the tip of the iceberg:-

"... it seems reasonable to ask, if Mr. Dunne had been such a ready and willing source of funding, which other business figures have done likewise, albeit perhaps in proportion to the scale of their respective funding."

Charles Haughey did not attend the first week of the tribunal's sitting. Neither was he legally represented. Nevertheless, his role dominated the proceedings. On foot of Ben Dunne's evidence, that was corroborated in certain respects by other witnesses, a direct conflict of evidence had arisen as to whether or not Haughey had received £1.3 million from Ben Dunne or Dunne's Stores Ltd. Haughey had previously denied such payment. For instance, in his reply of November 14, 1994, to a request for a return of the money from the solicitors for Dunne's Stores Settlement Trust, Matheson, Ormsby and Prentice, he had stated:-

"As no such monies have been paid no repayment arises."

Haughey was no stranger to this type of scenario. It had occurred perhaps most notably in the context of the arms trial in 1980, and again in 1982 in relation to his knowledge of the phone-tapping of political journalists. On each occasion, his version had been contradicted, sooner or later, by individuals of stature.

A psychopolitical dimension was introduced to the tribunal proceedings with evidence given by Dunne's Stores boss, Margaret Heffernan, on April 26, 1997. Mrs. Heffernan was represented by William Fry, solicitor. She testified that, having been told by Michael Irwin, the company accountant, that her brother, Ben Dunne, had given £1.1 million to Haughey, she confronted the latter at his home in Kinsealy in mid-1993.

M. Heffernan

"I said it had come to my knowledge that my brother had given him £1.1 million. He was totally relaxed about it and he said: 'I can't be responsible for what your brother says.'"

Denis McCullough, counsel for the tribunal, asked why Haughey had said this.

M. Heffernan

"... He said he felt my brother was unstable. That was the line of the conversation."

D. McCullough

"Was he indicating that your brother could not be trusted?"

M. Heffernan

"Yes."

D. McCullough

"Did you ask him if he got money?"

M. Heffernan

"Yes. He neither confirmed nor denied it to me. He actually avoided the question. He kept going back to the stability of my brother."

Thus, Haughey, a lawyer and an accountant, as well as a politician, exercised his facilities as an amateur psychiatrist when asked a question about a substantial sum of money. At the very least, it seems odd.

An Irish Times MRBI poll published on May 9, 1997, showed that, among a national quota sample of 1,000 electors at 100 sampling points, a clear majority - 65 % - believed Ben Dunne's evidence to the tribunal that he had paid £1.3 million to Haughey. Only 8 % believed Haughey's version of events.

The payment to politicians tribunal will run its course, having been adjourned for at least one month on April 28, 1997. Its disclosures accelerated the enactment of the Electoral Act, 1997. Its interim report was laid before parliament on May 13, 1997. A number of conditional conclusions have already been reached by those who have followed its progress, and who have considered the implications of the evidence to date. An Irish Times editorial of April 26, 1997, captures these well:-

"If the evidence given by Mr. Ben Dunne is correct, Mr. Haughey was a kept man. The Gandon mansion, the island, the yacht, the paintings and objets d'art *were not sustainable on his known income or accumulated wealth. He needed cash from the head of one of the country's largest grocery chains to make ends meet. And if he needed £1.3 million from Mr. Dunne in 1987, one must ask did he need other sums from other people at other times? If so, who were they and what did they give? And can we afford to make the comfortable safe assumption that they would all have acted as Mr. Dunne declares he did in handing over their subscriptions with no strings attached?"*

Similar questions arose in my mind shortly after it became clear that there was state involvement in the attempted cover-up of the abuse at Harvard in 1987. The evidence given at the payment to politicians tribunal has made these questions compelling. It transpires that, at the time of my confinement at Malden Hospital, Massachusetts, on foot of the sonic abuse at Harvard, Haughey's current account with Guiness and Mahon was overdrawn to the extent of £261,000. He *urgently required* money at that time and a plan evolved to approach a number of wealthy sources to obtain it. Indeed, the first payment Ben Dunne claims he made was by cheque dated December 1, 1987, for £182,630 sterling.

The tribunal has not heard the names of the other sources, apart from Ben Dunne, who were listed as prospective donors to Haughey in 1987. There has been speculation. For instance, Goodman International, the affairs of which gave rise to the beef tribunal in 1991, was seeking up to £90 million in 1987. In May, 1987, Haughey became directly involved in the negotiations between the company and the state. He had several private meetings with Larry Goodman thereafter between 1987 and 1989. It transpired that Goodman International acquired an immense amount of state benefits. By reason of the foregoing, in the Irish Times of April 25, 1997, Fintan O'Toole has remarked that:-

"It would be interesting to know whether Mr. Goodman was ever asked to be part of the alleged consortium of donors."

There is a similar rationale for my corresponding question, namely, whether Harvard was asked in 1988 to contribute to Haughey's financial well-being. Harvard was looking for a fix in 1987. A private corporation, with a $3.5 billion endowment, and an annual budget then of some $650 million, it could certainly afford it. Events in the meantime - many of them during Haughey's final term as prime minister between 1987 and 1992 - prove that significant segments of the Irish state apparatus, including U.C.C., and the taxing master's office of the High and Supreme Courts, have been fully committed to supplying that fix. These events have occurred in the context of a visit by Haughey to Harvard in 1988.

A very substantial benefit has accrued to both Harvard and U.C.C. arising from the fix - neither has been obliged to pay compensation for the personal injuries caused in 1987. Moreover, as an obvious result of political interference, U.C.C., with Harvard, has been allowed to withhold about £.3 million, including interest, of my property owed under the Supreme Court costs order of July 9, 1992. All signposts regarding that interference point to Haughey. For instance, the late Tom O'Connor, before at least seven credible witnesses, made clear on February 1, 1993, his design to reverse that Supreme Court order in his capacity as taxing master. The links between Haughey and O'Connor are well known. For instance, in *The Boss*, the authoritative work on Haughey's 1982 government, the authors, Joe Joyce and Peter Murtagh, note that:-

"Nobody was closer to Charles Haughey than Pat O'Connor

... the two families treated each other's homes as though they were their own."

The late Tom O'Connor, who purported to reverse the Supreme Court costs order, was a brother of the Pat O'Connor referred to in *The Boss.*

My suspicions that Haughey was the political linchpin for the U.C.C.-Harvard cover-up began in 1988 after I learned he had been invited to visit that university. Such was the evidence that accrued in the following years that, by 1993, the abuse of the taxing master's office by a close associate of Haughey was a hardly necessary confirmation of that which by then had become virtually obvious. The only real outstanding questions related to motivation. Even in 1993, the sleaze interpretation had the inside track. It has to be borne in mind that compliance with the Supreme Court costs order has no personal cost implications for either U.C.C. administrators or the staff of the taxing master's office. Charged on U.C.C., the order is to all intents and purposes payable by the state, out of public funds. Therefore, the most reasonable explanation for the political directive to seek to reverse that order is that the person issuing that directive would *gain personally* out of the vast combined treasuries of Harvard and U.C.C. Compliance with the order would mean that the fix had failed in the amount of the costs owed - a figure that now stands at some £.3 million including interest. In such event, the universities would end up paying twice, namely, the compensation, pension and costs owed *as well as* the political graft and the legal fees paid and payable to the intermediaries entrusted with effecting the cover-up. This would have been anathema to those involved.

The evidence received by the payment to politicians tribunal strongly supports the foregoing sleaze interpretation of events in the taxing master's office. In contrast with the image that he had projected, it transpires that Haughey was in desperate need of substantial finance in

1987, and was actively canvassing for gifts in consequence. A deal with the Harvard and U.C.C. interest group may well have been part of the rescue package. This financial analysis offers the most logical explanation of why about £.3 million is presently owed under the Supreme Court costs order of July 9, 1992, against U.C.C., with Harvard.

Neither the claim nor the sum involved is speculative. Both are based on a *judgment debt* established by the highest civil court in the state in the following order:-

> "AND IT IS ORDERED that the Respondent do pay the Applicant his costs (limited to expenses and outlay properly incurred) of the proceedings in the High Court and of this appeal when taxed and ascertained."

Based on extensive proofs, made available to the taxing master's office, the costs incurred were professionally certified on February 27, 1993, at £210, 871.84. James Flynn, taxing master, ultimately on December 3, 1993, issued an interim certificate for only £6,137.82. He was purporting to allow less than 3% of the costs incurred, in comparison with the normal allowance rate of 83% that was identified by the Denham report of 1996.

In purporting to misappropriate £204,734.02 of my property and that of others who had supported me in the five years of litigation against U.C.C., with Harvard, Flynn remarked that:-

> "I don't need any authorities."

That keynote statement was made on June 10, 1993, before several credible witnesses, four of whom verified it by affidavit dated July 1, 1993.

At this time, although Haughey was no longer prime minister, he had been succeeded by Albert Reynolds, a close supporter. Moreover, the judges who took *seisin* of our complaints to the High and Supreme Courts - Lavan and O'Flaherty - were beholden to Haughey for their positions.

The fact that a political directive of apparent Haughey

origin existed in 1993 not to enforce a Supreme Court order has no weight whatever, either in fact or in law. The order still stands and, in the meantime, at 10% cumulative interest, for the five years from the date of the order to July 9, 1997, represents a total debt of £344,367.28. At the rate of 10%, the interest element in the following year would be £34,436.72. These figures convey both the magnitude of the financial implications arising from the Supreme Court costs order of July 9, 1992, and also that these have been growing substantially, rather than diminishing, with the passage of time.

The latter fact is significant. It helps to explain the abuses of the criminal law processes that began in 1995 shortly after Dermot Gleeson became attorney general, and five days after I received a trite letter from him disclaiming a function in either the matter of costs or compensation.

It is highly improbable that U.C.C. changed senior counsel after my initial sucessful 1986 High Court case against that body. Accordingly, it is almost certain that Gleeson also began to act for Harvard in 1987, and thereafter as attempts at a cover-up have persisted. Indeed, the appearance of Donal O'Donnell in the universities' legal front team in the High Court in 1991 is virtually a verification of this. Gleeson and O'Donnell have worked in tandem, or at least on the same side, on a number of occasions, including in the context of the beef tribunal between 1991 and 1993. Given that there are about one thousand counsel in the state, this type of coincidence is significant.

It is a matter of public record that Gleeson charged daily fees of up to £3,000.00 in respect of his work for Goodman interests in the beef tribunal that ran for about eighteen months. On the basis of their ability to pay, there is no reason why he would not have charged at least as high a fee rate to the U.C.C. and Harvard interest group in the years of the attempted cover-up after 1987.

At that rate, Gleeson, and indeed the rest of the legal

team, would have amassed a very considerable amount of money from university coffers by 1995 - without having achieved the result that was paid for. From that perspective, abuse of the criminal processes in 1995 - that is continuing - may have seemed, in some perverted way, warranted.

Such abuse of public office in the state, even in recent times, is in no sense novel. The *Dowra* affair in 1982 is a well known episode in point. It involved not only the issue of the abuse of political office for personal ends, but also the extension of this abuse into a second legal system.

The *Dowra* affair occurred during the nine months' government of 1982 that was led by Charles Haughey. He had appointed Sean Doherty, a former special branch officer, as minister for justice. Initial disquiet in some quarters at the appointment were fuelled during the terms of the government by allegations of improper political interference by Doherty with the police:-

"In Roscommon, there was widespread criticism amongst gardai about Doherty's conduct locally. Many believed they were unable to do their job ... Many people around Boyle were frightened and refused to talk about certain things on the telephone.

The feelings of some people in Dublin were little different. They spoke of noticing cars following them, increased garda activity around their homes and strange noises on the telephones."

The extract is from *The Boss*, the acclaimed book on the period by Joe Joyce and Peter Murtagh.

The basic facts alleged in the *Dowra* affair itself were straightforward. James McGovern, the main witness in an assault case against guard Tom Nangle, a brother-in-law of Sean Doherty, was detained by the RUC in Armagh, Northern Ireland, for about twelve hours on September 27, 1982, the day he was due to testify in the assault case in *Dowra*, a town on the border between Cavan and Leitrim in the Irish Republic. The case proceeded in his absence, and Nangle was acquitted. As Joyce and Murtagh wrote in *The Boss:- "It appeared to be the ultimate 'fix'."* They recount the Irish Times revelations in December, 1982, that:-

" ... *not only had the RUC headquarters in Belfast ordered the arrest of Jimmy McGovern after contact with the gardai but also that the order was resisted by an RUC Special Branch Officer in Enniskillen ... A second report ... revealed that garda contact with the RUC was initiated from Doherty's office in the Department of Justice.*"

Is the *Dowra* affair echoed by the resort to the criminal processes against me in 1995 in the immediate aftermath of the American Supreme Court decision in the case against Harvard? I have no doubt that the answer is in the affirmative. Moreover, I believe that in order to understand the developments in the litigation that has stemmed from my claims against U.C.C. and Harvard, it is necessary to focus on the financial interests of the intermediaries. Until these are identified - the personnel as well as the amounts involved - the serial scandal will inevitably continue.

Since my litigation with U.C.C. began in 1986, I have been subjected to over sixty court attendances, listings or hearings directly arising from the abuses within U.C.C and Harvard and the cover-up strategies of the bureaucrats.

The procedural abuses have obviously been exceeded by the substantive ones. Notwithstanding proofs and admissions of the personal injuries case against U.C.C. and Harvard, I have still received no compensation through either the Irish or American legal systems. Whatever else it may be called, a system that does not provide compensation for injuries in such circumstances can scarcely be called a system of *law*.

I have also received neither an apology nor compensation for the brutal assault on me in the garden of my own home by the Irish police on May 20, 1995, or for the unlawful arrest and wrongful imprisonment at that time.

Moreover, my Supreme Court Costs Order of July 9,

1992, against U.C.C. with Harvard, presently represents an estimated £344,367.28, including interest.

Against this background, it would be risible to suggest that either the rule of law or constitutional justice has pertained or is pertaining. What is suggested, rather, is a more or less privatised *Buddy System*, as well as personal greed and financial interests on the part of certain individuals.

The perverseness and capacity for evil of the university personnel and their establishment affiliates that are recounted in this book were first recorded in the public domain of the Irish legal system in 1986, That system, and its American counterpart, have promoted rather than terminated the evil in the intervening twelve years. There is virtually a serpentine quality to the progression. This book has told nothing but the truth. A defence of ignorance is no longer available. Moreover, the failure of the rainbow coalition government to recapture its electoral mandate in the general election held on June 6, 1997, could well mark the end of the political stranglehold on the serial scandal. The new government, one hopes, will not perpetuate the abuses of its predecessors. Composed of an alliance of Fianna Fáil and the Progressive Democrats, and supported by a number of independents, that government took office on June 26, 1997. Its two leaders, Bertie Aherne, prime minister, and Mary Harney, deputy prime minister, had taken strong positions on standards in public life during their election campaigns. Moreover, in 1993, Robert Molloy and Pat Cox, both then members of the Progressive Democrats, when that party was in opposition, had made written representations in relation to the implementation of the Supreme Court costs order of July 9, 1992. They had been lied to in the replies from the taxing master's office. Robert Molloy was made a minister in the new government announced on June 26, 1997.

As in celtic mythology, the treasure may well be found at the end of the rainbow.

Postscript

On July 9, 1997, after this book had gone to printing, in a dramatic episode, Charles Haughey admitted that he had lied earlier to the payments to politicians tribunal. In a statement read to the tribunal by his counsel, Mr. Eoin McGonigal, S.C., Haughey conceded that he had received £1.3 million from Ben Dunne. He stated that he had *"mistakenly instructed"* his legal team on the matter.

These shock revelations immediately reverberated through the political system. Fine Gael tabled a parliamentary motion seeking a new tribunal of enquiry into payments by businesses other than Dunnes Stores to Mr. Haughey. The labour party leader, Dick Spring, said that the lower house should consider *"this extraordinary day in Irish politics"*. Mr. Bertie Ahern, Prime Minister, said that the government would decide what was necessary after it had seen the tribunal report. He would *"cover nobody. We will deal with this report comprehensively"*.

The date of Haughey's U-turn under pressure was highly significant for me. It was the fifth anniversary of my Supreme Court costs order against U.C.C., with Harvard, that had been won after a vicious and gruelling five year campaign. Defiance of that order had been initiated and maintained by a faction that was close to Haughey. Developments on July 9, 1997, suggested that the withholding of my property that had taken place might now come under public scrutiny. As Longfellow wrote, - *"Though the mills of God grind slowly, yet they grind exceeding small"*.